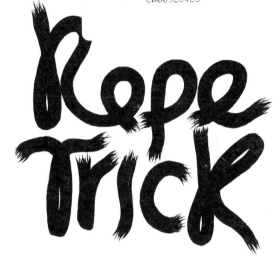

by
Ann Ruffell
and illustrated by Joanna Roberts

HENDERSON
PUBLISHING LTD

Chapter 1

To make a horror movie seemed such a good idea at the time.

There were five of us in our group, Gemma, Lee, Paul, Helen and me. And this was our Media Studies project. Our Parents' Association had just bought the school a whole heap of camcorders and the teachers wanted to show we were using them.

But whatever amazing idea we thought of, someone else had already thought of it before us... and written it down and given it in to Mr Parker. So there was no way we could argue we'd thought of it first.

We'd racked our brains over the last three weeks, and tomorrow was the deadline. If we didn't have an idea of our own by then Mr Parker would give us one.

And his ideas were the deadliest, dreariest ideas you've ever thought of.

"Jason's group have already thought of it, Lizzy," said Paul gloomily, coming back after a long queuing session outside the staff room.

I had been sure no one could possibly think of doing a movie about my own brother's pop group. I had forgotten one of the band has a brother in our class.

"What about a horror movie?" said Helen suddenly. She undid her long blonde hair from its scrunchie, let it drape over her face, and began to intone, "Double, double, toil and trouble..." Her fingers clawed and scratched at the air in front of her.

"Oh, brilliant!" approved Lee.

"Fantastic," said Gemma. She always agrees with Helen anyway.

"Ace," said Paul.

"Don't be stupid," I objected. "We've got to do something - well - sort of serious. Like a documentary. That kind of thing."

"Who said?" Helen shook the hair free from her face and began to tie it back again. "We've just got to make a film, that's all. Nobody said a word about a documentary."

"That's right," said Gemma.

"They don't care, as long as we learn how to do cutting," said Paul.

They were all crowded round me, like a coven of witches.

And I knew they were right.

But I had a funny feeling about it. If anyone had asked me what sort of funny feeling, I wouldn't have been able to tell them.

I made one last effort.

"But the others have all got things to film. Places, things - people to interview. We'd have to make the whole thing up - write a storyline. You know what we're all like at writing stories!"

Gemma giggled. "You'd think we'd copied each other, the way we all came last in the story-writing competition!"

"That's only because none of us are any good

at writing that kind of story," said Helen. "I never read science fiction."

"You never read, full stop," pointed out Lee. I knew he didn't read either, apart from car magazines.

"So we can't do it," I said, glaring at them. But I knew I wasn't going to win. Now that they'd got hold of the idea, there was no way they were going to let it go.

Paul went back to queue at the staff room door and just made it before the bell for the next lesson went.

"Parkie says that's fine," he reported triumphantly.

I couldn't help my feelings, but as the day passed by I forgot my forebodings and got caught up in their enthusiasm too.

Every spare minute of the rest of the day (which included the boring bits of science while we were waiting for our chemistry experiment not to work as usual), we thought up ideas for our movie.

"A row of corpses, all with their throats cut!" hissed Lee, right in the middle of Maths.

It was that sort of day. And we still had Spanish to look forward to! Monday was like an ongoing horror movie for me, one that happened regularly every week.

"Where are you going to get the corpses from?" hissed back Helen crossly.

You could see Lee was spending the rest of the lesson working out where he would get a row of corpses from. The teacher had to shout at him five times before he came to.

Gemma, the only one of us who was good at Spanish, looked up all the gory words she could think of in her dictionary. Words like 'fear', and 'terror', and 'death'. The sort of words which expressed the way I felt about Spanish. But I couldn't see that nasty words in Spanish were going to be much use in a horror movie. Nobody except her would understand them.

"Spiders!"

Helen shouted this in my ear, right at the end of Spanish.

"As if this lesson isn't bad enough," I said. "But I suppose they'd be easy to get hold of."

"No," said Gemma, shuddering.

"No!" said Paul decidedly. "If you have spiders I'm definitely not part of this movie. I'd rather make one about marketing."

We all groaned. Our group agreed weeks ago that marketing was the most brain-crunching topic we have ever done.

"No spiders, then?" said Helen, disappointed.

"No!" yelled Gemma and Paul together.

By the end of the day I was beginning to feel ragged - like I always do on Mondays.

The only good thing about it was that nobody seemed to be getting any really workable ideas for this movie that we'd all agree on.

It was a good thing because my jittery feelings began to get bad again. Like stomach aches do.

All five of us live quite near each other - Gemma and I in the same street, Helen two streets away and the boys next door but one to each other across a small park.

Gemma, Helen and I straggled across the pavement. Usually the last thing we ever want to talk about, just after a long day of lessons, is school, but Helen and Gemma just couldn't stop.

"Dismembered bodies..."

"Ghosts in the park..."

"Monster worms..."

And behind me, I could hear the two boys throwing out even wilder ideas, until I wanted to scream.

"Listen!" I bawled. I had to make them see sense. "There's no way we could film any of these things! We've only got two weeks before we do the cutting. Two weeks to get all our filming done. How are you going to do monster worms, tell me that, without a Hollywood special effects department?"

"Lizzy, you're a real killjoy, do you know that?" said Paul.

"Well?" I said belligerently. "We've got to think of something we can do, or it will be back to marketing and interviews at Sainsbury's."

They saw my point.

Then Gemma said dreamily, "A lock of hair. A lock of hair, swinging from a rope on the ceiling. Hair that's been cut from a victim..."

A little wind gusted round the corner of the park and stirred a heap of autumn leaves into an eddy at my feet.

I felt a sudden chill.

Helen laughed, suddenly, harshly. "You're not getting my hair!"

Gemma turned to look at her. "A long hank of hair," she said in a spooky voice. "Dark hair. The skin still clinging..."

"Brilliant!" pronounced Lee. "Pity about my hair." He stroked his dark crop complacently.

"You're not going to scalp me either," I managed in a kind of squeak.

"No," grinned Gemma. "But my brother might lend us his, since it's for a good cause."

"Ben?" said Helen. "But he's got hair down to his waist! He won't cut that, even for you." She laughed. Gemma and her brother had a sort of love-hate relationship, depending on whether they agreed about the same TV programmes they were going to watch, the music they were going to listen to on the kitchen radio, or whose turn it was to wash up.

"He had it cut last week," Gemma told us. "He's going for job interviews, and they said at the Job Centre that he might have more of a chance of an office job if he got it cut. It's hanging up in his room. It really scared me when I saw it first, I can tell you!"

I could see it in my imagination, slowly swaying from the end of its rope.

"Why is it hanging up in his room?" demanded Paul. "That's weird!"

"He got attached to it - well, first he was

attached and then he was unattached, if you see what I mean, and so..."

Lee rescued her. "So ask him if he'll let go of it for our movie! And I've got another world-shattering idea..."

"It doesn't have to be world-shattering, only mind-shattering," grinned Paul.

Lee ignored him. "A mutilated teddy bear!" he said with ghoulish relish.

Gemma, Helen and I shrieked.

"Lee! How could you!"

"Gruesome!"

"Poor little thing!"

"See? It will work!" said Lee. "It'll be worse than a thousand headless corpses. People really care about teddy bears!"

"Except you," I pointed out.

"Oh, well - a man's tough!" he said, and laughed.

I tried to enter into the spirit of the thing. "What about a bone?" I suggested.

"What?" They hadn't got over Lee's teddy bear yet.

"A bone," I repeated.

"Whose? Yours?" They weren't impressed.

"Well - just lying there. On the table or something."

"Won't it look like something from the Sunday joint?" said Lee.

"All right, if you're so clever," I shrugged. With any luck I could get them to think all their ideas were so stupid that we could stop this and get on with something sensible instead. "Okay, let's do something about 'A Butcher's Day' or something like that."

"Wait a minute, though," interrupted Helen. "If the butcher could give us something like a leg bone - you know, something really long and sinister..."

"Bones aren't sinister," said Paul, bored. "Not unless there are hands attached to them, and I can't see you getting that from a butcher."

"...and with blood dripping from it!" shouted Helen.

"We'll go to the butcher and ask for a nice long bone and two pints of blood, please!" joked Paul.

They were startled when I yelled.

"No!"

"No blood?" Paul was disappointed. "Ought to be able to get blood, from the butcher."

I could feel tension rising in me. Why wouldn't they stop?

Lee saw my face. I don't think he understood what I was afraid of - how could he? I didn't know myself. Maybe it was all this talk about blood. But he made another suggestion.

"Messages over the radio," he said. "Threatening messages."

"What a brilliant story!" said Helen.

"Story?" I said. "We haven't made up a story at all. I said we weren't any good at stories. There's no way we can do this. We'll have to do something else."

"We've told Parkie now," pointed out Paul.

"We've got to do it."

Not if I had anything to do with it, we didn't. But there's no point in saying that to my friends. Once they had an idea in their heads it was impossible to get it out.

I'd have to go and see Parkie myself.

I wasn't scared at the thought of blood, or spiders, nor for that matter any of the other frightening things they were dreaming up. I read horror stories myself - the more the merrier.

I remembered the time Lee crashed into the corner of a window frame two years ago. Who was it who had to mop his brow and run for the teacher on duty because the others were fainting all over the place? Right. Me.

Spiders? Oh, yeah, I don't like them, but I don't get hysterical about them. There was a girl who had a pet tarantula. She came into school one day and showed us. I've never seen a classroom empty so quickly! Although I didn't actually touch it, I did look at it - before the girl waltzed off home with her box of terror.

Threatening messages? Does anybody really listen to what they say on the radio? I only listen to my favourite songs. As far as I'm concerned the rest is just waffle between the music.

So what was it that I was so frightened of then? I didn't know. I couldn't put my finger on it. I just knew that we simply couldn't go on with this crazy idea. I had to do something about it now before Parkie left school.

"Oh no," I cried, quickly inventing an

excuse. "I've forgotten something... my Geography stuff."

"You can borrow mine," began Gemma.

"And all those other things..." I gabbled. "Don't wait. Sorry, I'll have to run."

I did. Fast. Parkie didn't hang about after school much longer than we did. I know, because he often passed us in his car.

With luck, I might just catch him before he went.

My bag lurched on my back as I ran: faster than I ever do in athletics, and my chest ached with panting.

I made it.

Parkie was just coming out of the doors, his arms full of inky exercise books.

"Sir..."

He sighed. It must have been one of those days for him too. I felt sympathetic, but this was urgent.

"Yes, Liz?"

"This horror story idea. Look, we've changed our minds..."

Perhaps I should have thought up a more tactful beginning.

"Liz, I don't want to hear any more about it. I've been waiting for your project idea for weeks. As far as I'm concerned, a horror story sounds like just the right thing for you lot."

Sarcasm now. I couldn't win.

"But..."

"I don't want to discuss it now, Liz. You've

made your choice - at last. Just go ahead and get on with it."

Nobody could say I hadn't tried.

I trotted back. The streets around the school were empty: strange and unwelcoming, the way they always are when the rush of school pupils has gone. Today though, they felt threatening too, as if people were watching behind windows.

The others had gone. Only Gemma was waiting, kicking her heels at the corner.

"You didn't have to wait," I said brightly. "Thanks anyway."

"You didn't forget anything, did you," she said.

"Well...no," I said honestly. "I just thought...oh Gemma - I don't know - I just thought, if we could think of something else, I could tell Parkie we weren't going to do this horror movie idea. Now it's too late: he says we've got to do it."

I met Gemma's eyes. She felt it too. They were big with fear. Not the sort of fear we felt for spiders. That was understandable. I could cope with that. But something quite different.

As if we were doing something dangerous.

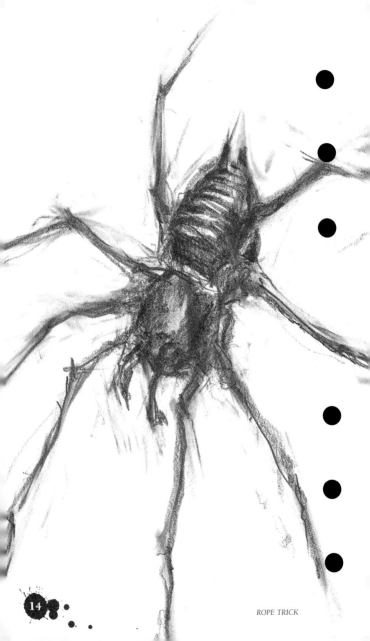

14

Chapter 2

Working on the principle that if you can't beat 'em, join 'em, I told Mum - enthusiastically - about our idea.

"I hope you don't think you're going to do it in here," said Mum sharply.

I looked round the kitchen. I could see what she meant.

It wasn't at all the right sort of place for a horror movie.

My mum is house-proud. You know the sort. Most of my friends' parents both work and they share the chores. If there's a bit of mess around they don't seem to worry. But though my mum works and pretends to share the chores, in reality whenever Dad or I do the vacuuming, or cook a meal, she has to come and tell us how to do it better, and will finish washing-up after us or re-vacuums when she thinks we're not looking. It was just the same when my brother lived at home and helped with the chores. And you just know that if you leave half a crumb on the draining board, Mum will have the spray cleaner out before long.

We haven't stopped doing our share, but we've stopped feeling guilty.

It turned out Mum's reasons for not shooting the movie in our house weren't the same as mine.

"Your Uncle Dave's coming tonight and I really can't have a horde of kids round my feet as well," she explained.

My Uncle Dave is Dad's brother. He's cool.

"Oh, great!" I said. "But he won't mind a horde."

"He might not, but I would," said Mum, leafing through a recipe book.

"Why don't you let Dad and me cook tonight?" I suggested. "You can talk to Uncle Dave instead - have a night off."

"Perhaps one day in the week," said Mum absently, searching for some fabulous feast to impress him with.

But it had made me think. Where were we going to shoot our movie? My friends' parents are pretty cool, as I've said, but I can't see any of them being very enthusiastic about bones dripping blood all over their kitchens.

Besides, how do you create the right sort of atmosphere from smart fitted cupboards and shining steel sinks? We needed a few cobwebs and peeling plaster.

I made myself a drink and a large cheese sandwich. Mondays make me very hungry. It's the stress of all my most unfavourite lessons coming together, and right at the beginning of the week. It completely spoils the weekend. You'd think they could have arranged things better.

"By the way," I said, my voice a bit muffled from the sandwich. "What's he coming for?"

"Does he have to have a reason?" said Mum. "Actually he's coming because he's bought a house near here."

"Ace!" I commented. "You mean, he's coming to measure up for curtains or something?"

That's what people seem to do when they've just bought a new house.

"Not quite," said my mother. "He's more likely to be measuring up for walls!"

"How come?"

"It's pretty much a ruin, I think. But a perfect place, he says - close enough to town to get in to his new job, and far enough out to seem to be in the country. If he bought something in good repair it would cost a fortune."

"Let's hope it doesn't cost a fortune to mend the thing, then," I commented.

Then it struck me.

"A ruin, did you say?" I asked carefully.

"Well - not as bad as that," said Mum. She stopped flicking pages and pressed her finger onto a colour picture with a satisfied grunt. "Ah - he's very fond of that!"

"I don't suppose he'd care if you gave him hamburgers and chips," I said. Then, as Mum began to look anxious in case I was right, I said soothingly, "but I'm sure he'll much prefer a - a - whatever it is you're going to do for him."

She stopped being anxious and thought about Uncle Dave's cottage. "As far as I can gather it's got four walls and the roof's in a pretty good state, but he'll have to do quite a lot of work inside."

Perfect.

We couldn't have thought of anything better

if we'd tried.

He arrived with Dad half an hour later, and I barely allowed him to sit down before I made my request.

"And, you see, it's on the bus route and not too far from anywhere," I said for the benefit of my parents. "We could take Lee's dad's mobile phone, just in case."

I wanted them to be sure we were all safe.

"Sure - if you like," said my Uncle Dave. "You can't damage anything, that's for sure. I get the keys tomorrow, so you could bring your friends to have a look, just to see if it's the right sort of place."

"It will be," I assured him. "Can we all come?"

"Lizzy!" protested my mother.

"No problem," said my uncle. "The whole point of coming to stay with you for a few days is to have a look at what needs to be done first - it'll be great to have some film of what it's like now to compare with what it will be like when I've finished."

But the strange, uncomfortable feeling that something was not right came back on Tuesday morning when I was telling my friends at school.

"It's absolutely perfect!" I enthused, to try and get rid of my crazy feelings.

"Tonight?" said Helen. She licked her lips in anticipation. "Shall we take the camcorder with us?"

"We haven't got anything set up..." I began, but Lee interrupted.

"If your uncle wants some pictures of this ruin, we can do that first, and start thinking about where we want to start our filming."

"Right!" agreed Helen and Paul.

There was no way I could persuade the others that they didn't have to take the camcorder tonight. There was no reason why they shouldn't - except my own feelings.

And maybe Gemma's.

I needed to talk to her, only it was difficult. We always went around in a gang at school. The others would wonder what we were up to if we walked off by ourselves: they'd think we were breaking up the group or something.

The only time we ever talked in a twosome at school was when we were planning someone's birthday surprise. And the person whose birthday it was pretended they didn't notice. We've always done that.

Today was nowhere near anyone's birthday.

And the others expected us all to be together as we planned our first movie scene. We'd grabbed our favourite corner of the quad. There's a bench there that everyone knows is ours, the one by the weeds and cobwebs.

"Gruesome cobwebs," said Lee. "We need to build up some spooky atmosphere."

"Without the spiders," said Paul firmly.

"How are you going to film cobwebs without spiders?" scoffed Helen. "But if you're so scared, I'll pick them all off and..."

Gemma screamed.

The trouble with Helen is that she gets really enthusiastic about things and goes a bit too far. She laughed, and let the spider crawl off her hand into the grass of the quad. But Gemma wouldn't stay on our bench any more, and we had to spend the rest of the dinner hour wandering around the field.

When I got home my uncle wasn't there.

Nor was anyone else.

Still, this wasn't anything new. As I said before, both my parents work, and though Mum sometimes gets home early, most of the time she doesn't, and I let myself in and make a snack if I'm hungry.

There was a note for me on the kitchen table weighted down with a heavy, iron key.

"Dear Lizzy,

I'll be back later than planned - I've got an interview with my mortgage broker. Go as early as you like, and make yourself at home with the spooks. See you there about nine."

My foreboding feelings seemed to have disappeared. I ran round to Gemma's and together we phoned Helen and the boys.

"Let's get there straight after tea," I said to Paul. "And don't forget the camcorder." I turned back from the phone.

Gemma waved the bus timetable. "We'll need this for coming back. I don't think I'll wait 'til your uncle comes at nine."

"I might go back with you," said Helen. "But I'd like to meet your uncle, Lizzy."

Did I feel another touch of chill? Of course not. It must have been just excitement at our project really happening at last. I shook myself. "You can meet him anytime," I said.

We saw the cottage from the road when we got off the bus. The long straight drive wound its way through two bleak fields. A single tree, half dead, stood starkly against the clear sky. Wilting leaves drifted from its branches. Grey stone walls crawling with lichen. A broken drainpipe clad in furry green moss where it thrived on the damp. Outhouses with sagging slates. A grey picket fence, its posts leaning crazily in all directions. Tall, ugly weeds choking the tiny garden.

A house to welcome the dead.

I began to shiver. Where had that thought come from? How could my uncle have invested in such a place.

We walked slowly - reluctantly - up the half-made road. The moon-like craters of the road were filled with slimy water, and edged with tired grass.

As we walked, everyone was silent. Silent as the grave.

The bus had disappeared over the brow of the hill. We heard its diesel engine fade into the distance. The sound of traffic was far off now. Our scrunching footsteps halted suddenly as we all jumped when a rook, cawing hoarsely, flew down from its nest and swept past us.

"It's like something out of a Hitchcock movie!" joked Paul.

We all laughed. It was a bit hysterical, but it was enough to relieve the tension.

"It's better than Hitchcock!" said Helen, her eyes gleaming brightly.

"If he's going to make this into a desirable residence, he's got his work cut out," said Gemma.

"Come on guys - let's go inside!" Helen urged. "Open the door Lizzy." She pushed me towards the forboding front door.

Shaking a little, I turned the key and pushed the door open wide into a mass of dust, cobwebs and gloom.

"It's incredible," whispered Lee.

"Perfect!" agreed Helen.

"Too many spiders," shuddered Gemma.

"True," said Paul, sidestepping one which ran across the doorstep. "Someone else can film them."

Helen began to explore. She had already marched us round the tiny front room, which had nothing in it but a broken chair. The next room, behind it, had probably been a bedroom, Lee thought. Helen kicked the remains of the door open.

It too was empty, with only peeling plaster on the walls.

But though Helen was the first one inside, she wasn't the one who fell through the floor.

Lee tested out a board that looked safe, put

his weight on it, and disappeared in a cloud of mouldy dust.

His head emerged, full of grey cobweb and splinters of wood. "Stop laughing!" he shrieked. "Get me out of here!"

"You looked so funny, though, disappearing like that!" giggled Gemma, taking an arm and pulling hard.

"It might have looked funny to you," said Lee crossly, dusting down his jeans, "but I could have broken my ankle."

"And stayed there all night, with no one to hear your screams, with only the owls and mice..."

"...and spiders!" Mischievously Helen broke in to Paul's scenario.

Gemma yelled, banged at her own arm in case anything might have crawled off Lee's sleeve, and backed away from the gaping hole in the floor.

"Come on," urged Helen, "there's a kitchen out at the back. And perhaps some nice creepy outhouses, if we're lucky."

We all stopped short at the kitchen door.

A rope was dangling. Right in the middle of the ceiling.

Underneath, a stool lay on its side. My eyes can see it still: a wooden stool, with a round seat and four legs braced with four bars. Lying as if someone had just kicked it over.

And a splash of red on the floor.

ROPE TRICK

Chapter 3

It must have been only a few seconds before anyone spoke, but it felt like years. We were just stuck in the doorway, staring.

"Well - there really is a bit more here," said Paul nervously.

"A bit more what?" Gemma's voice wobbled.

"Well - a bit more - sort of - atmosphere."

"You're telling me!" said Lee. "Floors that let you down as soon as you step on them, then a complete hangman's kit in the kitchen."

"Don't!" said Gemma sharply.

"Well - what else could it be?"

"Don't be silly," I said, trying to keep my voice steady. "There must be a reason for it to be here."

"Such as?" said Gemma.

"Well - " I struggled to find one. "People used to hang their hams from the ceiling, didn't they?"

"Did they?" Lee sounded doubtful.

" 'Course they did," said Helen. "Look - there's a hook up there, specially."

"I don't see why there's a rope, though," said Gemma.

"Because someone's been here and rigged it up to scare us," said Helen, laughing. "Wouldn't you?"

"No," I said violently.

"Yes, you would," contradicted Helen. "That's what we're going to do, isn't it? Hey -

one of the other groups hasn't decided to do a horror story too, have they? And got here first?"

"They can't have," I said. "We've got the key."

I took it out of my jeans pocket, where it had been wedged uncomfortably against my thigh ever since we had let ourselves in, and showed them.

"Well - it can't be too difficult to break in," said Paul. "Look at the way Lee fell through the floor. You could just as easily fall through the doorways."

"Just kids like us. Having a joke." Lee nodded his head.

"We'll have a joke on them," giggled Helen. "Gemma - you're the best at filming. Want to do a shot of the rope and stool before we move anything?"

"No, don't!" I said violently.

"Lizzy," said Paul plainly, "either you shut up saying 'don't' or go and do something else on your own. Except," he added hastily, "tell your uncle we'd still like to carry on, please. This place is awesomely spooky!"

"Okay," I said. "But when it all goes horribly wrong, don't say I didn't tell you."

"What could go horribly wrong?" said Paul. "Come on, Lizzy, you're just making things up. Unless," he looked at me slyly, "you're trying to work us up to the right sort of state of fear for the film."

"That's probably what I'm doing," I mumbled. Paul was right. It did seem silly to get all scared about something we were trying to make scary!

Gemma had the camera rolling. We stood out of the way while she filmed the rope hanging quite still from the ceiling, then moved the viewfinder to the floor to take the fallen stool. She walked backwards, so that both of them came into the frame.

"What about the blood?" reminded Lee. He pointed to the splash of red on the floor, which now that we had looked closely was simply a dollop of red paint. We've got splashes just like it all over the floor under our carpets where my brother tried decorating one year.

"It won't look so good after that," objected Gemma.

"Don't be stupid. The whole idea is to learn cutting," said Helen. "We can take pictures of anything and chop them up afterwards."

"That table'd make a nice chopping block," mused Lee as he rounded the once white scrubbed table, pushed against the wall.

"Don't talk about chopping up!" said Paul, and shuddered.

I felt like saying 'I told you!', but he had already opened the big wooden cupboard door with a noisy creak.

"Oh, my God!"

Inside the cupboard was a skull.

Helen laughed. "It's only a sheep's skull, you pathetic freak!"

"Well…" Paul looked shamefaced. "I mean,

it's not the sort of thing you expect to find in a cupboard, is it?"

"It's my bone," I said, fascinated.

"Not quite," said Helen kindly. "You wanted a nice long bone, with blood dripping off it. Not a skull."

I stared at her. "I didn't say what kind of bone. It was you who said that."

"It doesn't matter who said it," said Gemma. "I'll film it. Paul - open the door again - it makes a brilliant creaky noise - we can watch the door gradually opening."

She settled the camcorder against her shoulder and watched through the viewfinder. Paul shut the door, with an even noisier squeak, then opened it again, taking his time, so that the noise set your teeth on edge.

The skull grinned at us.

Gemma grinned too. "Great!" she said. "This cottage is practically writing our horror movie for us, Lizzy!"

"Okay - tell me what happened," I challenged her.

"It hasn't told me everything yet," said Gemma. "How about - well, the person who used to live in this house..."

"Man or woman?" interrupted Lee.

"Man, of course," said Gemma, at the same time as Helen said, "Woman!"

"Make it one of each," said Paul hastily as they looked as if they were about to quarrel. "A married couple..."

"No," said Lee. "Brother and sister. Always good for a few quarrels."

"I don't quarrel with my brother," protested Gemma.

"Not much, you don't," I said sarcastically.

"Well, not enough to..." Her voice trailed away.

"To what?" said Helen. "To murder each other?"

"That's not a murder. That's a suicide," said Gemma, waving at the fallen stool.

"But there's no body!" came a spectral voice.

We all jumped.

Gemma grabbed my arm. I saw Helen's mouth open and stay that way.

"Uncle Dave! For goodness' sake! I thought you weren't coming here 'til nine?"

My uncle looked automatically at his watch. "I was quicker than I thought. Just a few minor points which we sorted out in no time. Well - what do you think of my new house?"

"Brilliant!"

"Spooky!"

"Ace!"

"You're not going to make it like new?" This was from Lee.

"Well," said my uncle, "perhaps not quite new, but I do like some floor to walk on."

"Well - er -" began Lee, looking guilty, "I sort of..."

"Tell me the worst!" said my uncle, clapping his hand dramatically on his forehead. "I can take it!"

"He fell through the floor," I said plainly. "But it wasn't his fault. He's really saved you the trouble of falling through it yourself. I mean, if you'd been here, on your own, without anyone to haul you out..."

"I could have been here for weeks," agreed my uncle. "Shouting vainly for help, wasting away from lack of food. When you next came all you'd have found was a skeleton!"

"Hey!" said Paul with respect. "Want to write our script for us?"

My uncle shrugged. "You can have that part of it for free."

Gemma looked at him narrowly. "You wouldn't know anything about a skull, would you?"

"Skull?" said my uncle innocently. "What kind of skull?"

"Or this rope?"

"And the fallen stool?"

We clamoured round him.

"Okay, okay, I confess!" he laughed. "I thought you might like some really good things to film. Sorry I couldn't find a real human skull, but they're not available at the butcher's at the moment."

"Yeuch!" said Gemma with feeling. "Don't talk about butchers! They were going to go and ask for real blood!"

"Why not?" said my uncle. "Good idea."

"Why didn't you tie a loop in the rope?" asked Helen.

"I thought I had," said my uncle, looking at

the dangling rope critically. "But if I did, I can't have done a very good knot. It probably worked itself loose."

"I'm very glad it did," I said decidedly. "A proper noose would have been the absolute end! I'd never have come here again. Like that, you could think of some really good reason for it being there."

"Like what?" challenged Paul.

"Well - I'm sure I'd have thought of something eventually. Something really good - like the hook for hanging hams on."

"Oh, is that what it's for?" said my uncle, going over to look. "I suppose you're right. I thought it was for hanging a lamp on. There's electricity here now, but there wouldn't have been when the place was built."

Ham, or a lamp. Of course these were the logical reasons. But you can use things for wrong purposes.

Although my uncle said he had set up the rope and stool, and the sheep skull in the cupboard, I was beginning to feel uneasy again. There was something... but I couldn't determine what. It wasn't the rotten floors. It wasn't the rope or the skull, although they had made me jump.

Perhaps there was something about the cottage itself? But how could there be? I'd had these feelings about the whole idea, before I even knew about the cottage.

I tried to say something about my feelings to Gemma as we walked round the outside of the cottage. Uncle Dave pointed out the structural things he wanted to change, and Lee, Paul and Helen, their heads tipped back on their necks as they stared at the roof and guttering, made what they thought were clever comments.

Gemma doesn't know anything about building. She's always the one who knocks a nail into the bench instead of the thing she's supposed to be making, or stitches her fingers when trying to thread up the sewing machine. I don't know how she's so good with a camcorder: you'd expect her not to know which end of the camera is which. I might have been interested in my uncle's ideas at any other time, but not now. I needed to talk to Gemma because she seemed to be the only person who had felt the way I did.

"Perhaps it's the house," said Gemma. "It really is scary, even without your uncle's sheep skull!"

"But it can't be," I protested. "We felt scared before..."

"Who felt scared?" Gemma's eyes were blank, and I felt a chill of real fear.

"I was," I said bluntly. "And you were, too."

"Was I? Well, perhaps a bit, once."

"Why?"

"Oh - I dunno. You do, sometimes, don't you?" She turned and smiled. "Just from nothing, don't you? It's only like a sort of nightmare - or daymare."

But I don't feel fear like that. I've never felt frightened for no reason before in my life.

"I still don't think we ought to do this," I said stubbornly.

"Oh, come on, Lizzy," said Gemma impatiently. "You're making this up. The bits we've done so far are brilliant. And if your uncle thinks up some more grisly ideas..."

"Hey, Lizzy! Gemma!"

The boys were calling us to the outhouses.

"How about a scene here," said Lee enthusiastically. The slates on the roof were all tipping down from the broken ribs of the roof beams, as if they had been shuffled like a giant pack of cards and had frozen in mid-fall.

"Great!" I said, trying to work up some enthusiasm. "Can I have a go with the camcorder?"

Well, there wasn't anything wrong with the video camera. The tumbledown outhouse looked just the same through the viewfinder as it did for real.

"My turn next," said Lee. "I'm going to do a slow zoom from the top of that rise down to the cottage."

"The light's going," said Helen.

I hadn't noticed it before; it had been a bright evening, so that even inside the cottage the sun coming through the windows had been enough to light Gemma's film of the kitchen. But as Helen said it, we all noticed the chill in the air, the clouds creeping up from the horizon tinged by the dying sun with strange purples.

"Shall we go?" I wanted to go home and

switch on the TV and watch something amazingly normal, like *Neighbours,* though we'd missed that for today.

My uncle came back from the other side of the cottage.

"The light's going," he said, exactly the same as Helen. But somehow from him it seemed reasonable. "Want to see anything more before you go, or shall we make tracks?"

"Home," I said. "Please."

"I've got homework to finish," said Gemma.

"Me too," said Helen.

"Done mine," said Paul.

"Didn't have any," said Lee.

How can you not...?

But we're not all in the same set for everything, so it was just as likely, though not fair, that Lee shouldn't have any when we had loads.

"How did you manage that?"

As we drove home, crammed into my uncle's big estate car, we talked about our homework, next week's sponsored run, where we were going for half term, and everyone's ideas for the storyline of our horror movie.

"There used to be a family in this house..." began Gemma.

"Father, mother, and two point four children..."

"Is the point four a dismembered body?"

"Yeuch, Lee - do you have to be so disgusting!" shouted Gemma.

"It is a horror movie!" Helen reminded her.

"I don't think I want it that horrible!"

"Do you want a horror movie or do you want a horror movie?" said Paul cheerfully. "Anyway, this family - they move into this cottage, when it's all nice and new. But what they don't know is, the builders have walled up someone who insulted them..."

"The walls aren't thick enough for that," said Lee.

"Well - behind the fireplace, then. And plastered over it. In the night, the family hear this knocking sound..."

"The kids first," said Gemma. "They wake up in the night, and think it's a tree banging against the window."

"There aren't any trees," I objected.

"That's why they know it isn't a tree," said Gemma. "So they keep on having nightmares about it..."

"And daymares, later..."

Gemma gave me a sharp look, but didn't comment.

Lee went on. "Then the parents begin to hear the noise, and there's the sound of footsteps, walking right round the walls..."

"Hang on," said Helen. "What about the stuff we've already filmed? There's nothing about a rope and someone hanging..."

"All right," said Paul hastily. "This person got strung up by the builders, and they shoved the body in the walls to conceal the crime..."

"Great, Paul!" approved Lee. "Then we go

on with the banging sounds. We could do that tomorrow - pan round the walls."

"Oooh! Technical, even!"

"Are we coming back tomorrow?"

"Is that okay, Uncle Dave?" I asked.

"So long as you've done your homework," he answered with a grin. "I don't want to be the next one walled up by all your parents!"

When we arrived back at our house, Gemma said hesitantly, "I don't want to be a pain, but do you think we could watch the bit we've already filmed? Just to see if it's okay? You can't see it properly in the viewfinder playback."

"Yeah - please!"

They all wanted to come in and watch before going back to finish homework.

"Lizzy?" My uncle looked at me.

"Oh, Mum and Dad won't mind," I said. "There's not much - only a few minutes, really."

It was our good luck that my parents weren't actually watching anything they minded about. They went off to the kitchen to make coffee and talk about my uncle's plans for the building work, while Paul fixed up the wiring so that we could play back the little cassette over our TV set.

"Ready?" He sat back on his heels.

"Action!" we all cried.

"Ready for instant stardom!" said Helen.

Paul switched on.

The film moved through splintered floor-boards, artistic cobwebs, and peeling plaster.

"Great atmosphere!" approved Lee.

Then the scene jumped to the kitchen.
The rope hung from the ceiling.
But it wasn't still any more.
The rope swung, slowly, from the ceiling.

Chapter 4

"There must have been a draught," said Lee for the tenth time on Wednesday.

We were sitting on our bench in the sunshine. Frightening thoughts seemed miles away.

At least, that was what the others felt.

"Honestly, Lizzy, it's the only explanation," said Paul.

"But Gemma didn't see it move when she was filming," I repeated stubbornly.

Gemma was beginning to be convinced by all the arguments. "You can't see that well in the viewfinder," she explained. "If I was concentrating on something else, I could easily have missed a little sway."

"But you weren't concentrating on something else. You were concentrating on the rope," I said.

"If it had tied itself into a noose, I could see your point," said Paul, "but it was only the same old rope. Lee's right. It could have been a draught."

"What else?" said Lee.

"Or a malevolent spirit!" laughed Helen.

The others laughed, easy now in their explanations.

I didn't laugh.

Perhaps Helen was right, and there was a malevolent spirit somewhere about.

I didn't like to think about it.

They'd already moved on to talking about the next scene. "Can you get your brother's ponytail tonight, Gemma?" asked Helen.

"I asked yesterday, and he said it's okay as long as he gets it back," said Gemma.

"Don't anybody use it for dreadlocks," warned Lee.

"It's only you that needs any extra!" said Helen. "Okay, guys - what about the rest of the story? Honestly, we really need a storyboard, or we're going to waste loads of time filming things we won't use."

"How about filming you with your hair all over your face?" suggested Paul. "No - all three of you - Macbeth's three witches!"

"Thanks very much," I said. "And dangle Ben's ponytail over your face for a fourth witch?"

"Listen, you lot," said Helen impatiently, "like Lizzy said in the first place, we've got to have a storyline. There's no point doing all these images if they don't fit into a story."

"Fine," said Lee, jumping up from the bench and waving his arms about dramatically. "Give us the story, then."

"Well - what I think is, we've started with this idea of somebody walled up in the cottage..."

"And the kids are getting more and more worried about it," said Gemma, frowning with concentration.

"Who's playing the kids?" asked Lee.

"Not you," said Helen. "You're growing a moustache already."

"First you say I haven't got enough hair, then too much..."

"Paul, then."

"So you think I'm babyish," said Paul, trying to look insulted.

"And Lizzy for the other one," said Helen.

"Me? But I can't act!" I protested.

"You don't have to," grinned Lee. "Just look your usual self."

"How do you mean?"

"Well, you always look as if you don't know what's going on."

"It's a defence mechanism," I told him. "People always think they have to tell me, so it saves me from listening in the first place. But I wouldn't be any good. I look terrible in photographs."

I didn't want to be part of it. Suppose the film made me do something different?

I had to believe in that draught, but somehow I couldn't. And the uneasy feeling of fear grew inside me.

"What about Ben's ponytail, then?" I demanded in a kind of squeak. "Where does that come in?"

"They cut it off the victim, so that the rope fitted him better," said Helen ghoulishly.

"Perfect!" cried Paul. "And one night, when the banging got really loud, the kids come downstairs and see..."

"There aren't any stairs!"

"Okay, the kids come through from their

bedroom and see..."

"...the rope, swinging, with Ben's hair stuck onto it!"

"You'll see, Lizzy, when we actually make it move, it won't look at all the same as when it's in a draught," said Lee.

"Don't say it's Ben's hair," I said superstitiously. "You might find him walled up next."

"Don't be silly, Lizzy," said Gemma. But she had that look of fear in her face that she had denied having before.

"Where's your sense of humour, Liz?" said Paul lightly.

"We can do some good scenes with Lizzy and Paul listening at walls and looking frightened..."

At least that wouldn't be too difficult to act! Paul was right. I had certainly lost my sense of humour - at least as far as this horror movie was concerned.

It was time to go back into the school building for our afternoon lessons, but on the way home we finished working out what we would do this evening.

"I'll do the knocking on the wall while Helen pans round with the camcorder," said Lee.

"Why not me?" said Paul.

"Because you're an actor!" grinned Lee.

"Tell anyone who wants my autograph to join the queue," said Paul, taking a comb out of his pocket and running sweeping strokes through his hair.

"You're supposed to look scared, not glamorous," Gemma told him.

"This is just for the publicity photographs," said Paul.

"And then we'll string up Ben's ponytail and set it swaying," said Lee. "We should have time to do all that before the bus home. Unless," he said hopefully, "your uncle's going to give us a lift back again?"

"Sorry," I said. "He said he wouldn't be around tonight - that he'd have had enough of tumbledown houses after chasing builders all day today. He's leaving me the key, though."

"I hope he doesn't leave any more booby traps," said Gemma with feeling.

"Me too," I said. "A joke's a joke."

And then I thought perhaps it had been Uncle Dave who had set the rope in motion while we were filming. We didn't actually know how long he'd been watching us before he spoke.

A practical joke.

That's all it was.

Just like the rope itself and the skull.

I almost convinced myself. Except that when I found he wasn't there and wouldn't be back at our house until the next day, so I couldn't challenge him, my sense of unease came back.

I needed to know.

Perhaps if nothing happened tonight I would.

"I've left it behind!"

Gemma searched frantically through jeans

pockets, jacket pockets, and all the zipped pockets of the backpack that she was carrying the camcorder in.

"No hair?" said Lee dramatically, clapping his hands to his head. "And I needed Ben's lovely locks to keep me warm!"

"They weren't going to be put anywhere near your greasy head," said Gemma. "Oh, where on earth did I put it? I don't believe it!"

"Never mind," said Paul. "We've got lots to do with the tapping and me and Lizzy being film stars." He took the camcorder out of its case and squinted through the viewfinder.

"Never mind? He'll kill me if I've lost it!"

"Then we'll use your corpse as part of our film," said Helen, laughing.

"Don't say things like that," I said involuntarily. "Sorry Paul, but it's just asking for trouble."

"We're not in trouble, only Gemma," said Paul, moving the camera round. "Don't worry, we'll only use Gemma's corpse."

"You're absolute ghouls!" I protested in anguish.

"Great!" said Paul, taking his eye away from the camera. "Who said you weren't good at acting?"

"You didn't film me?" I yelled.

"Best shot of the film, I bet," grinned Paul. "Real fear. Brilliant!"

"Wind it back and record over it," I ordered him, trying to snatch the camera from him.

"Honestly, Paul, you're so awful!"

"No," said Paul, pulling it away from me. "It was good - wasn't it?" he appealed to the others.

"Fantastic," said Helen. "Why don't you get your revenge, Lizzy? Take a shot of Paul looking scared."

"If somebody doesn't take that rope down I probably will," said Paul, looking at the still-dangling thing critically.

"I tried," said Lee. "I can't undo the knot. Your uncle must have been a Boy Scout or something to do it as efficiently as that."

"Here, Lizzy. Have a go. See if you can make Paul look screamingly scared." Helen thrust the video camera into my hands.

I grabbed it, feeling more angry than scared now at the way he'd taken advantage of the way I looked. "Okay, then - look terrified, Paul!"

"It ruins my image," he protested. "Can't I even comb my hair first?"

"No!" said Gemma. "In fact - " she scraped her hands on the peeling walls and rubbed plaster dust into his hair. "There - now you look as if you've been investigating and don't like what you've seen." She rummaged in a pocket of her backpack and brought out a small mirror. She held it up in front of him. "Have a look."

"Absolutely ace!" I said, trying to keep the camcorder steady through my laughter. We all know Paul's really vain - he didn't need to pretend.

"You can't use that bit where he's looking in

the mirror," objected Lee.

"It's the horrified face when he looked up that we can keep," I said, grinning.

"Oh, all right," grumbled Paul, trying to shake the plaster dust out of his hair.

We spent the rest of our time recording the tapping on the walls. Lee tried several sounds: fists, knuckles, fingers, and a small log we found outside, and on different surfaces, while Gemma moved the camera slowly round to suggest this was where the noises were coming from. The sound doesn't come out on the playback through the viewfinder so we'd have to find out which sounded best when we got back home.

"Let's take a last shot at the rope before we go," said Helen.

"Why? It looked really good swinging like that."

"It's not swinging now," pointed out Helen. "It might prove it was the draught."

"Or not," I said mistrustfully. "I don't think we should..."

But I was too late. Helen had already filmed several seconds of the dangling rope.

I'm sure I watched closely. The others were sure, too.

That rope did not move.

"I'll tell Uncle Dave to get the darned thing down," I said. "I don't want to meet it every time we come here."

"I'm beginning to get used to it," said Helen.

"Well, I'm not."

"It could be really effective," went on Helen, "if we had them both - once swinging and once still. Or the other way round."

"Got the key Lizzy?" Paul had just looked at his watch. "Because if we don't go now we're going to have to walk home. Or be here all night."

Clouds began to come up over the back of the fields, clouds that were beginning to be tinged with evening purple.

"Funny - we've had some really strange looking sunsets this week," said Lee as we clambered over the back fence of the weedy cottage garden, making a short cut to the road and the bus.

"They're often like that," said Helen looking over in the distance.

"Well, I've never seen them," protested Lee.

"That's because there are too many trees in the way looking out from your house."

"Trees? You're lucky to have trees. All we have is houses," said Gemma.

But it was odd. I don't remember ever seeing such purple sunsets either and I could see sunsets from my bedroom window. Pink and red sunsets. Never this strange purple.

I shuddered, looking at it.

It seemed to symbolise everything I felt about this horror movie. There was something not quite right about it.

"Okay if we look at it on your TV again?" asked Lee when we got off the bus at the end of our road. "I really want to know which of those tappings worked best."

"Sure," I said.

I wanted to look at that rope.

If it didn't sway, I'd believe in that draught from yesterday.

Or believe it was my uncle playing games!

We set in the jack plugs and switched the camcorder to replay the stuff we'd filmed this evening.

"Hey, Lizzy - you're really good!"

"Call that good?" I said indignantly. But even I was surprised at how afraid I looked on the screen.

"Worth an Oscar!" grinned Helen.

"Better than me!" grimaced Paul. He didn't really look as horrified as Gemma had intended he should. He only looked annoyed at what she had done to his normally immaculate hair.

"Now for the really brilliant stuff," said Lee. "Steven Spielberg special effects department."

We listened to the various sounds, stopped, started the film again, rewound, argued, and made a final decision, only by this time Lee had forgotten how he had made that particular tapping noise!

And then, just as we were about to switch off and the others go home, the rope came into view again.

That last shot of Helen's.

She was right. It wasn't swinging at all.

But tied to the end of the rope was a long ponytail.

48

Chapter 5

"It's my uncle!" I blurted out. "It's got to be."

The others sat in shocked silence.

"I can't see how..." began Lee.

"It's impossible," said Paul firmly. "I was watching all the time, to make sure the rope didn't move."

"Me too," said Helen.

"Well, it hasn't moved!" said Gemma in a hysterical hiccup.

"Perhaps there's something on the film," said Lee hopefully.

"Either we're all seeing things or there's something funny going on," I said, trying not to let my voice tremble. "If it's my uncle, I'll never forgive him!"

"But how could he...?"

"He could have rigged something up," I said, desperate to believe it. "Something with mirrors or something. He did it before..."

"Not with mirrors," said Lee.

"There aren't any," said Helen flatly. "No mirrors. We'd have seen them."

"Well - you know what I mean - a trick or something. Like he did with that swinging rope."

"You think he did that?" asked Gemma.

"He said so, didn't he?"

"He didn't say he set it swinging," said Paul thoughtfully. "But I suppose he could have."

"What I want to know is," burst out

Gemma, "where's my brother's ponytail? He'll kill me, I know he will! I had to take it back tonight. I thought I'd left it at home, but I can't have done if..."

Her eyes filled with tears.

"Oh, come on," said Helen, "it's not that serious."

"It is!" insisted Gemma. "You don't know how much he minds about that stupid bit of hair! I was only allowed to borrow it if I took it right back tonight!"

"Well, you can," said Paul. "If you left it at home, that's where it is."

"How can it be?" shrieked Gemma, pointing to the now blank TV screen. "It's there! It's on the film!"

Lee's calm voice broke in. "We'll play it again. See if we can find out how the trick's done."

A trick. That was all it was. My uncle playing a trick.

Silently we wound back the film, watched my own face full of fear, watched Paul's horror as he looked in the mirror, which no one found comic any more...

And saw the rope, dangling, with the tress of hair quite plainly knotted onto it.

There was no mistake.

"I can't see how he's done the trick," said Paul, staring close up to the screen. "This film's a bit hazy - I can't see that well."

"I don't like it," burst out Gemma.

"Don't be silly," said Helen, picking up the

remote and snapping the TV off. "It's only a film. Anyway, you wanted to be frightened, didn't you? It's supposed to be a horror movie!"

"Yes, but you're not supposed to be horrified if you're making it," said Paul.

"I bet all the best writers and film makers are scared out of their wits while they're writing them," contradicted Helen. "If you're not frightened, how can anyone else be?"

"Yes, but..." I began.

"Tell your uncle it worked," said Paul with an attempt at laughter. "And ask him how he did it. I'm really amazed. I can't see..."

He sat on the carpet, close to the screen of the TV, zapped the remote again, rewound a short way, and put it on pause to stare intently at the trembling still.

We were mesmerised. Was it really Ben's ponytail? Or something my uncle had rigged up.

I didn't want to remember that I hadn't told my uncle about our plans to use Ben's hair.

"No," said Paul at last. "I can't work it out. He's really clever."

"I wonder how many more clever ideas he's got up his sleeve," burst out Gemma bitterly.

"I'll talk to him," I said, unable to keep my feelings of dread at bay any longer. "But I don't think it's him. I think there's something evil somewhere!"

"Don't be stupid, Lizzy," said Paul, sitting back on his heels. "You've got all wound up because you think it's your uncle trying to scare us. Just tell him that he did - really well! And if he's got any more special effects ideas, we'd like to know so we can put them in next!"

"But count me out if he has," said Gemma. "I don't like special effects that walk off with my brother's ponytail!"

"I bet it's at home," said Lee comfortingly. "Where you left it."

"It had better be," said Gemma, getting up to go.

But it wasn't.

Gemma rang me in a bit of a state about half an hour later.

She'd searched the house. There was no ponytail. And her brother would be home any moment.

We didn't mean to go to the cottage on Thursday, but Gemma insisted. Her brother took it a lot better than she expected, but as the image of his hair had come out on the film, she said it must be at the cottage.

"We could do the teddy bear bit tonight," said Lee.

It was lunch time again. We were on our bench in the quad. I was desperately trying to finish a bit of Maths that I'd forgotten to do last night.

"I don't want to do any more filming," I said. "There's something really nasty about that place. I want to look for Ben's hair then run out as quickly as possible."

"What did your uncle say?" asked Gemma anxiously.

"He didn't come back last night," I said shortly. My head buzzed with the problem of these numbers that wouldn't come out right. "I won't see him till tonight."

"But he was at the cottage yesterday, wasn't he?" urged Gemma. "He had to be, or how could he have done it?"

"Sure your brother didn't have anything to do with this?" said Paul suddenly. "It was his hair! He could be having you on."

"You should have heard him last night when I told him I'd lost it," said Gemma shortly.

The numbers suddenly came out properly. I scribbled down the answer.

At least you knew where you were with numbers. They were safe. Not like films.

I tried to keep my mind on Maths, but Gemma nagged, "Was he there?"

"My uncle wasn't at the cottage yesterday," I said defiantly.

"Wasn't...?"

"At the cottage," I finished for Lee. "Dad had the key with him all day."

"Perhaps it's the film," said Lee brightly. "Images moving where they shouldn't. It must be a fault. Shall we get another one? Tell them we've used up all that cassette?"

"Images don't just move by themselves," I replied. It was this that was bothering me, but we could try another film anyway to see what that might prove.

"I'll get one while I give in this Maths. If I'm lucky he won't have picked up the rest of the pile."

"So we can do my teddy bear!"

"You're not having one of mine!" yelled Gemma.

"Nor mine!"

"Nor mine!" grinned Paul.

"You don't still take a teddy bear to bed, Paul?"

"I'll bring my own, then," said Lee huffily. "Only I haven't got one," he explained.

"Good," I said. "Leave it that we just look for Ben's hair, and get out?"

Perhaps we could make a movie out of the bits we had already. Film the rest at home. Or out in the street.

I didn't want to go back to that place any more than I had to, even if it was the film that was causing us problems, and not the cottage.

I had changed the film. But I couldn't change Lee's mind.

It was almost inevitable that when we passed a skip on the way home he had to look inside it.

And even more inevitable that he should find a teddy bear in it.

An old, battered teddy bear, with one eye missing and half its stuffing spilling out of its stomach.

"No, Lee!" I whispered as he dragged it triumphantly out of a box of broken toys.

"Brilliant!" he crowed, holding it up. "One mutilated teddy bear! Did you remember the film, Lizzy?"

"Yes," I said dully. "But I don't think we should..."

"We've only got another week after this. It'll get darker and darker. The light's not that good now. And the weather forecast says there's going to be rain most of next week."

All of Lee's arguments were convincing.

Except when you were already convinced that there was something terrible going on.

I hoped his theory about the cassette film was right. Although it seemed pretty unlikely.

As the bus drew nearer the cottage my feelings of fear grew stronger and stronger. If there had been any way of getting home once we were off the bus, I'd have gone straight away. But there wasn't another bus for an hour.

I had to stick it out.

"There, you see," said Lee when we stepped off the bus into a shaft of bright afternoon light. "There aren't any ghosties here, I promise you."

It looked so ordinary, quite plain grey stone, with all its roof intact, and a beaten path to the door. The garden was full of weeds, sure, but in the sunlight now, it looked the sort of place that someone might like to live in after all.

Not like a haunted house at all really.

We searched all over.

"Shall I knock on the walls to ask the ghosts where they've put it?" suggested Helen.

"No!" I said.

"Okay, keep your hair on!" said Helen huffily.

"Keep Ben's hair on, you mean," grinned Paul. "I can't see it anywhere. And let's face it, there's not a lot of places you can look."

It was true. Even the sheep skull had gone from the cupboard.

"Can we film my teddy bear now?" asked Lee plaintively. "The light's beginning to fade, but there's a good streak of light coming in this window and some good gloomy shadows in this corner. We could stick your scared faces just after it, as if the children have found it when they come to investigate the tapping."

"Great idea," said Helen quickly.

"We don't have to look scared again, do we?" I said superstitiously. If I had to do it again, perhaps something else dreadful would happen to make my fear for real.

"Look, if you like," said Lee, "but not for the film. What we've got will be perfect. Now if I lay it here..."

The teddy bear was placed so that the light showed up all the horrible tears in its stomach.

"It looks as if it's been stabbed loads of times," said Paul with satisfaction.

"Oh, stop it!" shuddered Gemma. "Poor little thing!"

We stood round as Lee photographed it from several directions, so that we could choose the best shot later on.

"Is that the new film?" I said suddenly.

"You should know," said Helen. "You brought it."

I felt in my pocket. The old cassette was marked with our names and HORROR FILM. We hadn't labelled the new one yet.

I breathed a great sigh. It was the right one.

"I'm not letting this injured body out of my sight," said Lee when he had finished. He stuffed the mutilated teddy bear back into the carrier bag he had brought it in. "Okay - nearly bus time."

I locked up, glad to be out of the house again, and we all trooped down the path to the bus stop on the other side of the country road.

At least my uncle couldn't have done anything untoward this time.

There had been nobody in or around the cottage. Paul and Gemma had kept going outside to look. I'd stayed with Helen to watch that it really was Lee's skip bear that he took out of the bag, and that it was put back into the same bag when he had finished.

And he didn't let the bag out of his sight until we were home and playing back the short piece of film on our TV set.

None of us could believe it when the rope appeared again.

Lee began to pick up the remote, thinking we had rewound too far.

But on the end of the rope dangled a mutilated teddy bear.

Screaming, I rushed for the bag.

Inside it was one of my own teddy bears.

The toy Lee had taken from the skip was nowhere to be seen.

ROPE TRICK

Chapter 6

I hugged my teddy bear close.

"It's one of you!" I stormed. "You knew I was scared! Making up all that stuff about my uncle. You knew it wasn't him - you knew it couldn't have been him, because it was you all the time!"

My mother came into the room.

"Anything wrong?"

She looked round at our tense faces.

"No," said Lee at last. "Lizzy thinks we've been playing a trick on her, but we haven't."

My mother caught a glimpse of the hanging teddy bear, frozen on the pause button. She shuddered. "Is this what they teach you at school nowadays?" she said disapprovingly.

"It wasn't like that," said Gemma. "It's just..."

But this was between us five. My mother couldn't help, even if I wanted her to.

"We were just having a bit of a row about it," I told her. "It's okay. We've finished now. You can have the TV."

"I'm not bothered about that," said my mother quite plainly. "But you mustn't frighten yourselves. This is an important year for you all: you can't let it take up homework time like this. I thought it wasn't a very good idea when you came home and told us, Lizzy, but I didn't want to interfere."

My heart was thumping fast, with

indignation that my friends could have done this to me, and with fright - because I think deep down I knew they hadn't. Any more than I had.

"This is our homework, Mum," I explained. "And we've all done our other assignments - haven't we?"

The others all nodded eagerly, though I happened to know that Gemma was two days behind with hers. Losing her brother's ponytail had really upset her.

"Well, I've got a bit of Geography to do, but I'll do that when I get home," said Lee.

"In fact, I'd better go too," said Paul.

The boys got up to go and walk across the park to their homes. Helen went too, leaving Gemma with me because she wanted to copy up some of the History that she hadn't done. We often do our homework together.

Mum seemed satisfied when she saw us settled at the kitchen table with cans of coke and our books spread out.

"There's a new gingerbread cake in the tin if you want some," she said. "Uncle Dave will be back later. Perhaps you can tell him how things are going with your film."

Gemma and I looked at each other.

"Sure, Mum," I said.

"It can't be me," burst out Gemma as soon as Mum had gone. "I wouldn't pinch my own brother's ponytail!"

She looked so upset that I had to believe her.

"Then it's got to be one of the others," I said stubbornly. "Nobody else knows about our ideas. I'm not going any more. I won't do it. If you want to join them you can, but I've had enough."

"I don't like it either," said Gemma. "You know I don't."

"You told me you were okay," I said sharply.

"I was trying to pretend I wasn't scared. But you're right. I was scared right from the start - just like you. I think it was just the idea of doing a horror story. Do you think everyone feels like that if they make horror films?"

"If they don't," I said darkly, "what is it that's making us afraid?"

"The cottage? Maybe something happened in it - something like the story we were making up."

I wanted to believe it was true. It made more sense than that my uncle or our friends would trick us so that we were nearly scared out of our wits. I mean, a joke's a joke.

"Perhaps Uncle Dave will know."

"What will Uncle Dave know?" He breezed into the kitchen, bringing the scent of outside with him. "What about a cup of coffee, then?"

I looked narrowly at him. But there was nothing in his face to suggest he'd been playing another joke on us and wanted to see our reaction.

We told him about our last two trips to his cottage, and tried to explain what had been happening on our video tapes.

"No," he said solemnly. "I certainly didn't set

that rope in motion, and I swear, too, that I had nothing to do with your teddy bear or your brother's hair, Gemma. For goodness' sake, what do you take me for anyway? As if I haven't got enough to do just sorting out the bank and the builders!"

"Well, is there some story about the house?" I asked. "Maybe somebody died, and wants revenge or something?"

My uncle laughed. "It would be impossible for someone not to have died in a house of that age," he said. "Are you trying to make me have nightmares in my own house? Come on, Lizzy. It's only an old house. And if there were any ghosties, they'd have run away years ago. There's not a lot going for them - it's been empty for ages."

"There you are," I said triumphantly. "They were just waiting for someone to come along to be haunted! Why hasn't anyone lived there? Tell me that?"

"Because nobody wanted it," said my uncle patiently. "It's too far out of town to be handy, too close to be in the country, and there aren't many buses, as you've discovered."

"But who was there before?" I insisted. Gemma leaned her elbows on the table to listen better, pushing her History aside.

"A perfectly ordinary family with two perfectly ordinary kids, as far as I can gather. They moved for a perfectly reasonable reason - Dad got a job in Canada, and the whole family emigrated. They kept the cottage in case it didn't work out so that they could come back if they wanted. What they should have done, but didn't, was get someone to be caretaker. That's what I'd have done. Or rented it out - though I think they tried to do that but as I've said the house is just a bit too far out of town for anyone to want it."

"But why is it falling down?" I asked.

"It's not," said my uncle. "It's simply deteriorated a bit because of neglect. See an empty house, and the first thing your ordinary yobbo wants to do is chuck a brick through the window. So the wet gets in, and nesting birds, and chilly animals, and before you know where you are you've got a wreck on your hands. Nice for me, because when they came over a couple of months ago they thought it was such a wreck that I got it for a really good price."

It all sounded so reasonable.

"Children, you said?" Gemma's voice was carefully controlled.

"Two. One of each. Well, if neither of you is going to make me a cup of coffee, can I make you one?"

Our eyes met across the table.

"How old are the children?"

"Almost grown-up now - in their twenties perhaps? I think they were about ten and twelve when the family went out to Canada. I don't know. Why? Is it important?"

"And they're still alive?" I said.

"Very much so," said my uncle, going to the tap and filling the kettle. "You can't make ghosts out of them, Lizzy. Sorry."

"I still don't like it," I said. "There's got to be a restless spirit there, I know it."

My uncle unhooked three mugs and poised a teaspoon over the instant coffee jar. "Want some?"

"No thanks," said Gemma. "I won't sleep."

"I can't sleep anyway," I said. "This film's giving me nightmares."

"Hot chocolate, then," said my uncle. He dolloped a spoonful of coffee into his own mug, then reached for the tin of instant chocolate. "But listen - perhaps you're getting the jitters because you're there in the evening. How about if I come with you on Saturday? I want to get the builders over tomorrow so that they can have a proper look on site, so I'd rather you weren't around then anyway. I can have a look at your film sometime and see if I can spot the trickery. How's that?"

"You think someone's messing about with the tapes? Maybe filming something before we do?"

"A rival gang?" laughed my uncle.

But I'd picked up that new tape from the school office this afternoon.

True enough, there hadn't been any wrapping round it. There never was, with the school ones.

It was just possible.

"I think Lee has a paper round on Saturday.

I'll ask," I said.

"I won't be up at paper round time," said my uncle. "No point in having a few days off if you get up at the same time as you normally do. How about straight after lunch, then you girls can go to town or do whatever you do on Saturday mornings?"

"No money," grinned Gemma. "Spent all my pocket money in advance three weeks ago, and I don't get any more till next week."

"I'm about the same," I admitted. "But Helen always goes to town, so afternoon will be fine."

My uncle wandered off with his coffee to work on his building plans. Gemma turned to me.

"Bit of a coincidence, two children," she said.

"Not really," I said reasonably. "I mean - there's two children in your family and two in mine. Boy first, girl second. Just the same."

"I wonder if we made them up." She stared down into her cup of hot chocolate.

"What are you getting at, Gemma? Of course we made them up," I said impatiently.

I was impatient because I didn't want to think she might be right. "In any case, they're grown-ups now."

She avoided my gaze and stared stubbornly down into her steaming cup. "There's definitely something wrong with that house," she insisted. "Your uncle says they came back a couple of months ago - with the two children - and that the children were in their twenties, but how does he know it was them? They could have been anyone."

"Don't be ridiculous Gemma," I said. "Of course it was them, coming back to sell the house."

"People don't," she said stubbornly. "They could easily have got an agent to sell it for them. You don't come all that way just to sell a wreck."

"They didn't know it was a wreck," I tried to reason.

"They must have known, if it had been left for that long," argued Gemma.

"Well I don't know... perhaps they came back to visit relations." I was fed up with this. Gemma drank the remains of her chocolate and began to tidy up her books ready to go. Then, with a conscious effort, she shook her hair back out of her eyes and grinned. "That cottage is getting to me," she confessed. "To be honest, I wouldn't mind if we never had to go back there again. Still, at least it'll be daylight when we next go there."

When Gemma had gone, I rang the other three. I suppose I wanted to sort of apologise that I'd thought they had jinxed the tape.

"My uncle wonders if it could be one of the other groups," I said to Lee.

"Possible," said Lee's voice over the line. "They must have monkeyed about with the camcorder as well, then, or it would have recorded over the top."

Not possible. Not possible. The words kept resounding in my brain.

"My uncle says it wasn't him," I told Paul next. "Could someone have messed about with the cassettes before we got them?"

"The security they have in that office, anyone could have got in and messed about with cassettes," said Paul. "We'd better keep ours chained up!"

Possible. The word tried to rub out that other word 'not'.

I called Helen and explained that my uncle Dave would come with us on Saturday.

"Is afternoon okay by you?"

"Sure," said Helen. "Listen, if I can't do spiders, what about blood dripping from the tap? The walled-up guy getting more and more squashed..."

"Helen!" I screeched so loudly into the phone that Mum came out of the sitting room to see what was the matter.

"Lizzy, now I've got to put my foot down..."

"It's okay, Mum," I said, though I could hardly stop shaking. "Really, it's okay."

But it wasn't okay.

Suppose someone had heard? Suppose someone was tapping our phone? It wasn't that hard, you heard about it all the time.

Or maybe someone could read our thoughts...

Chapter 7

Helen told Gemma about her idea on the way to school before I could stop her.

"For heaven's sake, Helen! Do you want the world to know? All these people going to work, going to school. Anybody could hear!" I looked round fearfully. Suppose the person who was playing tricks on us was creeping up behind - waiting to overhear.

Helen looked round elaborately. "There's nobody here," she said flatly.

And then with a kind of despair I knew that if my theory was right, whoever was either tapping our phone or reading our minds, would have known anyway.

The boys spent all their spare time on Friday wondering how they could get something red into the water tank so that it could gush blood-coloured water. They were so preoccupied that I couldn't hope to stop them.

I spent all Friday with my stomach knotted with fear, wondering what was going to happen next.

On Saturday my uncle came to the rescue.

"Sorry. At the moment the water's cut off, but that's not a problem. I need to turn it on some time to see if the plumbing works. But no red gunge in my water tank please! You want to poison me and wall me up for ever?"

We all laughed nervously and piled into his

estate car.

"First the bad news," said my uncle. "At least, it's good news for me though bad for you. My mortgage is all sorted out, and so are the builders. They've had some kind of hitch with the job they should be doing next, so they want to start on mine next week - which is fantastic news for me. So you won't be able to film for at least a fortnight, I'm afraid."

Relief rushed over me like a clean wave of seawater.

"Oh dear," I said insincerely. "The whole thing's got to be finished by then."

He looked at me with concern.

"No," I said hastily, "don't worry, it's all right. We've got just about everything we need, haven't we?" I appealed to the rest of them. "We don't really need blood from the tap!"

"Yes, we do!" said Helen indignantly.

"Well - perhaps you can put some food colouring in the sink and let the tap drip onto it. How would that do?"

"It's not quite the same as blood," said Paul.

"Can we stop off on the way and buy some?" asked Helen.

"What? Blood?" said my uncle.

"Food colouring," smiled Paul.

"We don't need..." I began, but Helen was adamant.

"It can't do any harm, Lizzy," said Lee uneasily.

"It's not a teddy bear," said Paul. "It doesn't matter if it disappears!"

"Has your brother's hair turned up, Gemma?" asked Helen.

"You know it hasn't," said Gemma sulkily. She turned to look out of the window and refused to talk any more.

"A dripping tap will do, really," said Lee.

"I want blood!" hissed Helen.

"What a vampire," said my uncle, laughing. "Supermarket?"

"Please."

He good-naturedly stopped at the local mini-market and Helen bought a bottle of some red food colouring.

"It doesn't look like real blood colour, but it might come out all right on the film," she said thoughtfully.

"I hope it doesn't look like real blood," I said fervently. "Everything on this darned film is too real for me."

"Lizzy, you're too sensitive," said Helen.

It should have been a nice thing for her to say, but it was an insult. You know when Helen's insulting you - there's a kind of look in her eye. She can say what you think are the nicest things - until you work them out afterwards. I wondered why I hadn't noticed this before.

We were all being nasty to each other at this point. Gemma went into a mood for the rest of the day. The boys started playing up, and rushed around the place like little kids, making a lot of noise.

My uncle looked as if he wished he'd never asked us. I couldn't blame him either.

"Does it feel creepy?" I asked him.

"Now you ask, no," he answered. "But what's up with you lot? I thought you were the best of friends?"

So did I.

"Oh - you can't be all friends all of the time," I said lightly.

"Are you all worrying about this film of yours? I'm sorry I never had time to look at it, but I'm sure it must be all a hoax, you know. Nothing to worry about. Maybe someone's so impressed by your idea that he or she is trying to stop you. What's the worst scenario they're working on in your class?"

I laughed tremulously. "I don't know. Everybody's gone deadly serious. They're all worked up about their films. We've only got two lots of equipment for cutting, so Mr Parker's put up a list - you know, we've got to queue. We're last, and people are complaining we've only got the best of it because we were so late getting started."

"There you are. A good reason for sabotage," said my uncle.

"I hope you're right," I said.

"Hope? Do you want people to mess up your film?"

"No," I said. "I'm afraid of what it is, if it isn't someone playing a rather nasty joke."

"Ghosts don't exist," said my uncle, laughing

at me. "You've got to believe that, Lizzy."

If only he knew how much I wanted to believe him!

You would have thought there was definitely some kind of nasty spirit around that Saturday, with us all snarling at each other. Even the red water in the sink didn't work properly. My uncle managed to turn the water on and we filmed the first few drips - then we heard the rushing sound of water in the bathroom and had to dash to turn off taps there. That wasn't all - even when we'd turned every tap off in the house, there was still the sound of dripping: the old pipes were leaking like a colander!

"I suppose I'll have to have the place re-plumbed as well," he said crossly. "Well, it'll have to wait till the central heating people come."

We rushed round with our coke cans trying vainly to stop the leaks flooding too much before my uncle yanked the tap shut again.

"What a waste - buying that food colouring," said Helen. She was clearly annoyed, as if it was all my uncle's fault.

"We don't have to do it here," said Paul. "Can't we do it in someone's kitchen?"

"Not mine," I said decidedly. "My mum's already refused!"

"Could try ours," said Paul. "Our kitchen tap leaks, too."

"Why didn't we think of that in the first place?" said Lee. "Much better idea!"

In one way it was a relief. I didn't want to

stay near the cottage any more. It certainly had a bad feel to it this time.

But I didn't want to carry on with our film either. We hadn't made up an ending to our story yet, and I was scared that whatever we thought of might start coming true on the video.

"Wait a minute!" I said, my mind still worrying, "I suppose it couldn't be the camera?"

They looked at me as if I'd gone completely off my trolley.

"What couldn't be the camera?" asked Paul at last.

"The things that keep happening. I've changed the film, and they're still happening. But what if it's the camera?"

My uncle looked at me, shaking his head. "Perhaps you'd better listen a bit harder in your Physics lessons, Lizzy. It's not possible. You know that."

Paul nodded his head, though I bet he doesn't listen any more in Physics than I do.

"We've got a camcorder at home. We could use that," said Helen, sympathetic for once. "That would prove it, wouldn't it?"

You could see my uncle was getting a bit impatient, as if we were trying to keep a good story going on for longer than anyone wanted to listen to it. I think he was really irritated about his leaky plumbing, too.

"Have you finished?" he said. "No more filming?"

"No, thanks," I said.

"But we don't know the ending yet," objected Helen. "We might think of something we've absolutely got to film here, and we won't be able to come back because of the builders. And after that it'll look too modern, as well as too late."

"What, then?" said Lee.

The atmosphere seemed to be getting to him as well. He was uneasy. I saw him glance at Gemma, who hadn't said a word all morning.

"Does the walled-up chap jump out of the plaster?" suggested Paul.

My uncle suddenly laughed. "The builders will be doing a damp course first - and that means tearing down the plaster! You could come and ask them while they're here if you like!"

Why did he have to think of that! And why didn't my uncle say "Certainly not!"

"Who's going to crawl out of the plaster?" I said in a panicky voice. "You do realise that if we film you doing that, you'll never come back again!"

Chapter 8

"What do you mean?" Paul's face was disbelieving.

"Where's Ben's ponytail? Where's the sheep skull?"

"Didn't you throw it out?"

"Did you? Who did?"

We all looked accusingly at each other.

"Uncle Dave?"

"No. I must confess I didn't," he said. "But there have been surveyors around. They've probably thrown it back into the field where I found it."

"And the teddy bear?" I insisted.

"Nobody would mind about that teddy bear," said Helen. "Somebody chucked it out in the first place."

"That's not the point," I said. "Where is it?"

"Look," said my uncle, "do you want to make a search for things you've lost, or can we go?"

We all looked at each other. Helen opened her mouth as if to say something, then shut it again.

"Shall we go?" suggested Lee.

"Okay." Everybody agreed.

"If you replay that film I'll see if I can think of any explanation for those unexplained moments," said my uncle.

"Thanks," said Lee.

Gemma pulled her hair over her face and huddled inside it.

Paul was sitting forward on the back seat, the seat-belt strained across his chest, staring out of the window as if there was something he badly needed to see.

Paul doesn't think things out. You have to point them out to him. So when things do zap into his skull they kind of hit him hard.

"Suppose..." he began.

"What?" I was eager to hear someone else's thoughts. Perhaps there really was a rational explanation.

"Oh - nothing." He lapsed back into gloom, jamming his elbow against the base of the car window and cupping his chin in the palm of his hand, to gaze vacantly outside.

I didn't want to replay the films when we got back. I wanted to destroy both of them. Burn them. Bury them twenty metres deep.

But what would happen if I did? Would Paul and I - captured on the second film - be suddenly ravaged by fire? Would we wake up in the morning to find ourselves in a grave so deep we couldn't ever be found?

Did Paul think we'd be the next people to disappear? Was that the reason why he was so tense?

He turned and gave me a weak smile.

"We're still here," I said.

"How long for?" he answered, and went back to staring out of the window.

"We've played it already, Paul," I said insistently. "The other things disappeared straight away."

76

Why was I bothering to try and reassure him?

I knew the answer. Because I needed reassuring myself.

When we arrived back at our house I could see Paul didn't want to sit in front of our films again. And Lee and Gemma weren't much better.

"Come on, Paul," urged Helen.

She was the only one of us who seemed to have nerves of steel.

"Yes - let's see what the jinx is," said my uncle.

"Back so soon?" said my mother when we trooped in. "You're just in time for cake."

There was a delicious smell of chocolate cake cooking in the kitchen, and a loaf of gingerbread already steaming on the rack. Mum likes baking - she says it helps her relax. Which is maybe why she's not too keen on Dad or myself being in the kitchen!

It was all real and tremendously normal. I ought to have felt good about it.

But the gingerbread might as well have been an old duvet for all I could taste of it. My mouth was dry and the cake fell into a kind of solid, painful lump in my stomach.

I glanced round at my friends.

They were nibbling little corners of their gingerbread.

We were all putting off the time when we'd have to look at our recording.

Uncle Dave wolfed down a second piece. Mum smiled with gratification. "What a good thing I made two," she exclaimed happily.

"Two chocolate cakes?" said my uncle greedily.

"Only one of those," said my mother, "and you'll have to wait for that: I'm going to ice it for tea."

"Wonderful," said my uncle, "I can wait. And while I'm waiting - let's have a look at that video."

He strode off to the sitting room, leaving us to straggle reluctantly after him.

Silently I handed him the first cassette, and we plugged in the camcorder.

We all watched quietly.

"You've got some nice effects there," he said. "So what's the trouble?"

"The rope, first," I said.

"The first one? Or the second one?"

"It was swaying. It is swaying."

"Was it? I didn't notice. Shall I rewind?"

"No," I said. "Go on."

He looked at me quickly, but I avoided his eyes.

"And you didn't knot that hair into the rope?"

"No."

"Sure?"

When people keep on at you like that, you start wondering whether you did or not.

"I don't remember," said Helen, as if she were in a dream.

"I don't remember either," said Paul.

"Nor me," said Lee, staring at the screen.

"What do you mean?" I said sharply. "Gemma? It's your brother's hair."

But Gemma had hidden herself in her hair

again and refused to look at the screen.

"What about the teddy bear, Lee?"

"I don't know," he said. "I simply don't know."

I wanted to shout at them, to tell them what they'd seen. What we'd all seen

But I began to wonder myself.

"Seems to me you're playing a little game with yourselves," said my uncle. "It's all very effective - is that what you want to know? Pretending you don't know anything about it to see if outsiders are scared? Well, so far you've succeeded. It's a nice, scary little video. Almost professional."

We should have felt flattered.

Perhaps the others did.

I simply felt dulled.

But my uncle had moved on to today's recording.

"I can't see why the pipes should have burst," he was saying crossly, watching the short seconds of dripping tap. "The water's been turned off ever since they moved to Canada. No wonder the stop tap was..."

"Oh, look!" said Lee.

Paul began biting his fingernails furiously.

Helen's eyes were fixed to the screen.

The camera had moved to the sink. And the splashes of water on the greyish white enamel were bright red.

Uncle Dave explained it away, of course.

"It's a trick of the light," he insisted. "One of you - was it Helen? - was wearing a red coat. I saw it hanging on the kitchen door. Easy for the light reflected from that to reflect back into the water. But it's another really great effect!" he said encouragingly.

"Thanks," I said, without meaning it.

"You should get some good marks for it," he went on.

"If we can cut it right," I said automatically.

"Well, if there's anything I can help with," he said vaguely.

"Thanks, anyway."

"Yes, thanks," said my friends as they went out of the door.

"I suppose there is an explanation?" said Paul on the doorstep.

"Must be," said Lee, but not as if he believed it.

"Weird," said Helen. She shrugged on her red anorak. "I suppose it could have been this. What do you think, Gemma?"

"I didn't look," said Gemma. "I don't want ever to look at it again. I don't want anything more to do with it. I don't care if we don't finish it. I don't care if I don't get any marks and miss out on a huge chunk of coursework. I don't want to know!"

"Oh, come on, Gemma!" said Helen. "It won't be fair for us to get all the marks you ought to have."

"We'll just play it the way it is," said Paul.

"Can't," Lee reminded him. "It's the cutting that's just as important."

"Helen can do that," said Gemma. "I've told

you, I don't care if I don't get any marks at all. You can do it all."

She rushed down our front path and along the bit of pavement to her own house.

There was a long silence.

"Well - see you Monday, then," said Lee.

"Monday," echoed Paul.

Helen shrugged and kicked her way down the road. I watched her go. Then I went back inside, before the boys had reached the park they had to cross.

I wanted life to go back to normal. What was the most normal thing I could think of?

"Have some cake," said my mother, "and have you got any homework?"

She was really startled when I hugged her.

"Yes," I said thankfully. "I have! Loads of it!"

You couldn't get anything much more normal than that.

I usually leave Friday's homework till very late on Sunday evening, when I'd remember it and have to rush to get it done in time, but today I settled down to it. Nice, normal Maths. Nice, normally horrible Spanish. I think I learned more words that night than I've ever done before.

You have to keep your mind concentrated hard on something else when there's something you don't want to think about.

At eleven o'clock the phone rang.

My parents had gone to bed. I was still working on my Geography project.

I rushed out to the landing to grab the phone before they were woken up.

"Lizzy?"

"Gemma?" I whispered. "What's the matter?"

"Lizzy - I was going to have a bath and..."

I heard her terrified breathing on the other end of the line.

"Gemma! Tell me! What happened?"

Her voice was tremulous, sobbing.

"Lizzy - I turned on the bath taps - and they ran red!"

Chapter 9

"And it wasn't coloured water," sobbed Gemma.

She was shaking so much she couldn't hold onto the glass of water I'd given her. It slipped through her fingers and crashed onto the carpet, leaking water into the pile.

"I'm sorry!" she cried, trying to mop the water with a tissue.

"It's okay, it's okay," I said, though I was shaking a bit myself. "Look - nothing's broken - it's only water. It won't matter."

"I turned both the bath taps on," she said. "It's so scorching hot you've got to let the cold in straight away - and then - and then - "

She couldn't go on.

My parents had heard the doorbell and came downstairs.

"Something the matter?" asked my father.

"Gemma turned her bath taps on and blood came out of them," I told him baldly.

"Oh, surely not, Gemma," he said laughingly. "With all these roadworks - the water board's working all along the street - we keep on getting rust in the water, and it looks exactly as if..."

"It was real blood!" said Gemma wildly.

"What a shock you've had," said my mother sympathetically. "I'll make us all some tea."

"But she's right, Mum," I said, trying to stop my voice from trembling. "It's this video of ours. Everything we say comes true. It's all happened on the film, and now it's happening for real when we're not even filming!"

"We've had discoloured water before, Lizzy," said my mother soothingly. "It's a bit of a shock the first time you see it, then you see all the little flakes of rust settling at the bottom."

"But it's all swirly, like blood!" cried Gemma.

"There there, Gemma," my father assured her. "Your imagination must have been working overtime. Would you like some tea? Or would you prefer a soft drink? Coke?"

"Coke, please," said Gemma in a muffled voice. She had buried her head in her arms. When she looked up again, I saw tears streaked down her face. "It wasn't food colouring! That's a sort of pinky red. This was real blood - thick...!"

"I'll get on to the water board first thing in the morning," said my father.

"But Dad...!"

My mother gave me one of her warning looks. "Let's get Gemma calmed down, shall we?" she said quietly.

"You don't believe us, do you?" I choked. "It's been getting worse, Mum. You just ask the others."

"Lizzy," she said impatiently. "Let's not talk about it any more, all right?"

"Can I call them and tell them?"

"Certainly not!" she said. "It's far too late."

I just hate that awful rationale she puts on when she thinks you're being rude. You just can't get through to my mum when she's like that.

"When she's finished her drink, I'll walk her back home. Will your mother be back soon, Gemma?"

"She's - she's..." gulped Gemma. Then she kind of pulled herself together with a huge effort and said, "She'll be back any minute. She'll be worried if I'm not there. Thanks. I'd better go."

Mum insisted on walking her to the door (so that she could stay with Gemma if her mum hadn't got back yet), but she was back within minutes.

"Now I want to talk to you, Lizzy," she said as soon as she was back inside. "This horror nonsense has got to stop. I know it's for school, and you thought it was a good idea, but it simply isn't healthy to get so obsessed with it. I'm going to phone the school tomorrow and..."

"You don't understand, Mum - "

"Maybe I don't understand, Lizzy, but one thing I do know is that you've been increasingly upset lately, and it can't go on. Dad will phone the water board tomorrow - or Monday, if they don't think this is an emergency - and we'll sort out Gemma's little problem with the water. But you've got to stop frightening yourself like this."

Me? Frightening myself?

If only that was all it was!

We met at school on Monday in a very sober mood.

Gemma hadn't walked to school with me that morning. I knocked, as usual, but her mum said she was a bit late and would come on by herself.

She kept away from us, as far as you can in lessons, until break, then as we walked uncertainly to our bench in the quad, she marched up, holding out the camcorder case.

"I'm not doing any more," she announced. "Here - you have the camcorder, Lee. Lizzy's got the cassettes. Just count me out from now on."

She left our bench and went off with some friends she'd had at junior school.

It was really strange without her there.

"Um..." began Lee.

"We need a kind of warning," Helen said. Gemma might still have been there for all she noticed. She was deep in concentration. "That'll just about wrap it up."

"Helen, how can you be so insensitive?" I protested.

"Don't say you're backing out as well!" she said.

"Can't we do something else?" said Paul.

"What else?" said Helen. "But this is the most brilliant idea of all. Besides, everyone else has thought of something worth doing, you know that. We've already tried - that's why we came up with this idea," she went on. "Martin's group are doing that stuff about cleaning up the canal. Abigail's group are doing the drama club production. Jinny's lot are doing your brother's pop group, Lizzy."

"If only we'd got there first!" I said with feeling.

"I'm sure I could think of something now," mumbled Lee.

"This late? We've got to do our videotape cutting at the end of this week. We can't!" said Helen. "I'm not backing out."

"I'll carry on," I said suddenly. I had to keep going. It was the only way I could convince myself that my fears were irrational. I had to see this through.

"Well, if we're going to finish this film, let's just do something where we don't have to go to the cottage," said Lee.

"We can't anyway," I reminded him.

They all looked relieved.

"No. We can't, can we?" said Paul. He laughed. "Unless we film a lovely ghost covered in plaster dust!"

"Don't!" It was Lee, not me, this time. "If you say something it's likely to come true! Don't you see?"

It struck me like a thunderbolt.

"It only happens when we're at the cottage!" I cried.

"Gemma's bloodstained water wasn't at the cottage," Lee reminded me.

"No, but we thought of doing it there. We had the food colouring there."

"Suppose," began Paul, "suppose that we think of something that's not at the cottage. Something we haven't even thought of doing at the cottage - wouldn't that prove it's the cottage that's causing all these things?"

I wanted to believe him.

If it were true, I could tell my uncle. And tell him to sell it again. Quickly.

I liked my uncle. I didn't want sudden bulges to appear in his new wallpaper, nor a strange zombie to come out of his wall during the night.

"I think that might prove it," I agreed. "Let's think of a way of doing a warning - like Helen says - only without going anywhere near the cottage."

"What about Lee's radio message?" Paul reminded us. "Suddenly a voice comes through, out of the blue, and gives out a threatening message."

"Just like they do when they say there's a twenty mile jam on the motorway!" said Lee.

"It'd be really easy to make that convincing," said Helen. "We could film your radio, Lizzy, then add the sound from a tape..."

"Why Lizzy's radio?" asked Lee suspiciously.

"Why not? Because we usually go to Lizzy's to play back our film. It doesn't matter. Use yours, Lee, if you like. What sort of a radio have you got? We'd need something that looks kind of old-fashioned."

"That's the story of my room," I said ruefully. "Everything there is old-fashioned, even my chewing gum!"

I described the radio. My Uncle Dave had given it to me, years ago, when I was a kid. It had all the stations I wanted, but there wasn't a tape recorder or anything. I had had a proper stereo system for my birthday last year.

"I thought you said everything was old-fashioned?" teased Paul.

"Well, everything except my new CD player!"

The jokes fell dead as dry leaves.

We stopped talking.

I think everyone felt they didn't want to go on with any more of this film, even if it wasn't at the cottage.

It was going to be bad enough cutting it.

"It must be something at the cottage," I said at last. "Do we really need to prove it by doing something else?"

"We've got enough material," agreed Lee. "We don't need to do any more. We can cut the videotape we've got and still make a good story out of it."

Helen got up from the bench.

"Well, if you don't want to do it properly..." she said, tossing her blonde hair back over her shoulders.

She walked off towards the school buildings.

The sky had been lowering all day, piling grey cloud upon grey cloud. As we watched

Helen reach the main doors, the first heavy drops fell.

☠

My uncle was to stay all the next week. Things weren't going as he had planned.

"There's always a hitch, isn't there?" he complained to my parents as we sat round the table after our evening meal. "Just as I've got everything nicely sorted out, the solicitor tells me I can't make any structural alterations without permission from the builders!"

"That's rather unusual, isn't it?" said my father. "I've heard of planning departments making this kind of condition, but not builders!"

"Strange, isn't it?" agreed my uncle. "With the place built so long ago, the builders would have been dead and gone years back!"

"In that case..." began my father.

"Oh, no. My solicitor tells me that if the firm's still going, I have to ask permission from whoever is boss now! And if it's not, he's got to find out who took over from the original builders. It's all a complete waste of time. I suppose there is one good thing: it means Lizzy's friends can go and film there if they like."

No! Just the thought of going near that place was enough to make my blood freeze.

Then what he had said hit me.

My stomach started to churn nervously.

The builders wouldn't let anyone make alterations. Not without their permission.

"Do you think..." my voice wouldn't stop trembling. "I mean - why should they say you can't do anything without their permission? Have they - perhaps - walled someone up in there!"

"Lizzy!" warned my mother sharply.

"It's this stupid video you're making," said my father angrily. "You're getting all kinds of silly ideas, Lizzy. If you could be sensible for once..."

"I don't think it would be a good idea for them to go back there, Dave," said my mother. "They're frightening themselves to death."

To death. Was that what the place wanted? For us to frighten ourselves to death? For once I agreed with my mother.

"I don't want to go there ever again," I said. My hands didn't seem to be able to keep still. I put them under the table, so that no one could see. "None of us wants to go there. And I don't think you should either! Uncle Dave, please sell it. Please don't live there. It's evil!"

"Come into the sitting room. Let's talk this through," said my uncle calmly.

Mum began to object, but Dad said, "Good idea, Dave. Talk some sense into her."

"It may not be the cottage, but there's something wrong," said my uncle. "She might find it easier to talk to me."

It was as if I wasn't there. I began to cry. "If you could take me seriously for once..."

I followed my uncle into the sitting room,

my face streaked with tears. "I do know what I'm talking about," I insisted.

The TV stood blankly in the corner. Images rushed through my mind. Perhaps it was the TV set? But, no, it couldn't be. I knew there wasn't anything wrong with the TV, or the film, or the camcorder. There was something - someone - bad, making these things happen.

Uncle Dave sat opposite me, looking sympathetic.

"It's still happening," I choked. "Everything we talked about. You remember we tried to film fake blood dripping out of the tap?" My uncle nodded. "And you know on the screen it looked as if the taps were dripping blood for real? And you said it was a trick of the light?" He nodded again. "Well, on Saturday night Gemma turned on her taps to run a bath - and it filled with blood!"

He came over and patted me on the shoulder. I tried to calm down.

"Your mum and dad told me," he said quietly. "Listen, I think we can settle this."

"We can?" I looked up expectantly.

"If I take some of that bath water to the lab and look at it under a microscope. Or you could do it yourself at school, if your teachers will let you. Then we'll know one way or another if it's real blood or if, as your Dad suggests, the road works are contaminating the water. Has she kept any of it?"

"Shall I call her?" I ran to the phone.

Of course she hadn't kept any of the red water. It was too much to hope for.

"But I'd like to come round, Lizzy," said Gemma. "My brain won't work properly - shall I help you with your Spanish? I feel..." she sniffed a little, as if she was fighting with tears. "Ben won't talk to me since I lost his ponytail. Mum's gone out with her boyfriend, and I'm feeling a bit lonely."

Me too.

"Don't worry so much, Lizzy," said Uncle Dave. "It's a pity I can't prove to you that all these ghostly things have got to have natural explanations. But next time - keep the evidence!"

"I will," I assured him. "But the cottage - Uncle Dave, really you mustn't live there! It's an evil place, I know it is!"

"I refuse to be pushed out of my own house by a ghost," declared my uncle. He smiled. "I bet I've got a stronger will than it has!"

"I hope you're right," was all I could reply.

"I don't want to talk about it, Lizzy," said Gemma when she had unpacked her books and arranged them neatly over the floor of my room. "I told you, I don't want anything to do with it any more. If I'd kept any of that bathwater," she shuddered at the memory, "I'd have been really pleased for your uncle to get it analysed, but I didn't, so we won't ever know. Can we get on with our Maths now? Please?"

"Shall I put the radio on?" I suggested.

"Good idea," said Gemma, and the strained

look she'd had on her face over the last week smoothed out just a little. "I could do with a nice blast of loud pop music!"

The song we tuned into on our local radio wasn't exactly loud, but it was one of our favourites. It was enough to blot out the worry of the last few days - for the moment.

The next song was another of our favourites, and we were both humming along to it when suddenly there was an interruption.

"I wish he wouldn't do that," I said crossly. I really hate it when disc jockeys talk in the middle of a song. "Why can't they just play the CD and wait until the end?"

"Wait. What did he say?" said Gemma in a panic-stricken whisper. Her face had turned deathly white.

"What's the matter?"

She put her fingers to her lips to silence me.

I listened to the voice.

"And that's the message."

"A request? Someone's asked for a request for you?"

Fiercely, Gemma slammed her hand over my mouth and shook her head.

"Here are the names again: Gemma, Lizzy, Lee, Paul and Helen. You have been playing a game called 'Rope Trick'. Remember, everything you think of is part of that trick. Everything."

There was weird music, and a hollow laugh.

"Including," went on the hateful voice, "this one!"

Chapter 10

"Well - a message from outer space!" joked the presenter, obviously flummoxed for a moment. "I don't know where that one came from! I hope you're listening, guys! A message from nowhere to tell you how to play the game of - of - " A faint voice said something in the background. "Of Rope Trick! And now back to Geranium Spy and their latest single..."

You could hear the surprise under his well-known laugh.

We sat rigid.

The song ended.

"Did you...?" whispered Gemma.

"No. We decided not to. We just talked about it, that's all."

Gemma was quiet for so long that I had to break the silence. "Look, it's one of the boys. It's got to be. I'm going to phone up the radio station and see who it was. I'm getting fed up with these jokes."

Gemma listened on the mobile extension while I dialled from the phone on the landing.

"It was a complete surprise to us as well," said the producer when I finally managed to get through to her. "Sorry - Lizzy, did you say? - sorry, Lizzy, but we've simply no idea how anyone managed to broadcast that message on our air waves. We've been checking all the tapes we've used, and checked all the studios, but there's nothing we can find. Do you know who it is? One of your friends?"

"I suppose it must be," I said. "I'll have to ask around."

"Do that. It's a complete mystery to us. If you do find out how they did it, let us know. It's a technique we could use!"

I nearly put the receiver down, when she said "Just a moment."

Then she came back on the line. "Sorry - that's Mike Daring - the presenter of your programme - he said he's checked the CD as well - seemed incredibly unlikely, but that's the first time he's listened to it, and these groups do odd things sometimes. As I said, he's checked it right through, and there's no message on the disk."

"Right. Right. Thanks. Yes, if I do find out..."

"Can I?" said Gemma grimly, pressing down the cut-off button as I replaced my receiver. "I want to get those guys!"

"Sure - help yourself."

She dialled Lee's number.

It was my turn to listen in.

"Don't be stupid," said Lee. "How could we? Sure I heard it. So did Paul. He's here now."

We heard the ringing of my front door bell without surprise.

Uncle Dave let Helen in. We heard her talking to my uncle in the hall, then heard her footsteps come up the stairs.

"Did you hear...?"

"Yes," I said. "So did the boys. We were all listening."

"How on earth...?" said Helen.

"The producer doesn't know. Nor does Mike Daring. We've just called the radio station."

"Someone's been clever," commented Helen. "Are they trying to scare us or something?"

"They're scaring me!" shuddered Gemma. She was playing with a sheet of her Maths homework, folding and unfolding the page and turning it back on itself until the squares fluttered apart.

"Well..." began Helen. "If nobody knows...?"

"Nobody. They said." I had a sudden thought. "Unless you...?"

"Me? I don't know anything about radio. You know that!"

We laughed, uncertainly.

"Only how to change stations," she went on.

"It's got to be one of us," I said, staring her straight in the eyes. "Nobody else thought of this idea. And we didn't even try to put it on the video this time."

"I didn't think of it," protested Gemma.

"It's got to be one of the rest of us four, then," I said, still looking into Helen's eyes.

They were blank.

I opened my mouth to ask her, straight out, but there was a noise at the door and the boys arrived.

"That's pretty cool!" said Paul. "How did they do that?"

Gemma went right up to Lee. "Was it you?" she demanded. "How could you! You know I'm scared out of my wits!"

"Me?" Lee looked startled. "No! How could it be? I just heard it on the radio, then Paul came round and said had I heard it..."

"And then you phoned, so we thought we'd come over."

"Since we're all here," said Helen, "why don't we look through our videotape again and see how we're going to shape the story."

We all looked at Helen as if she was mad.

We were all shaken. We didn't want to know about our horror movie.

She shrugged.

"We're all here," she insisted. "We've got to do it some time. It would save time at school."

"You don't think we're going to go on with it!" protested Paul.

"We've got to," she said calmly. "Come on, guys - Lizzy's got the camera and the film, so we might as well. The sooner we crack on, the sooner we can finish it."

"Sorry - count me out," said Paul. "In broad daylight, at school, I can cope, but not here. No, thanks. Got my homework to finish. Coming, Lee?"

Lee nodded, and they sloped off again.

It was quiet in our house. Only the faint sounds of the TV from downstairs and the tick and creak of our central heating system.

A sudden gust of wind blew my curtain

inwards. I felt the cold breath of air spill from underneath it.

Our house is old. The window frames don't fit properly any more. Even with the windows shut you get plenty of fresh air! I'd shut my bedroom window as soon as I went in it this evening.

"Okay - then let's just us look at it. All the way through this time, so that we can work out our storyline."

Why was Helen so insistent?

"We can't," I said loudly. "My parents are watching TV and I can't interrupt them."

"Come over to ours," said Helen, smiling. "We can use the TV in my bedroom."

I felt a chill in my bones.

"Helen, how can you!" said Gemma. Her voice cracked with nerves.

Helen turned to look at her. "Why?" she protested. "Look, I'm sorry, but I just don't get scared at horror movies or stories. I only wanted to see if everything had worked out all right, that's all. But we can do it at school, like Paul says."

Perhaps that was all it was.

Now I came to think of it, she was like that. If we put on a late night horror movie at a sleep-over party, the rest of us would be hiding under our sleeping bags, but Helen would either be screaming with laughter or trying to work out how they did the special effects.

I wanted to think this out.

"Sorry, Helen," I said.

"Okay." She smiled. That strange, blank

smile. "See you tomorrow, then."

And she was gone.

"Do you think I should change my idea?" I heard myself say. I felt strangely assertive - as if I couldn't help myself. "Change my idea about the bone, perhaps."

Gemma looked at me as if I'd gone mad. She got up from the floor where she'd been sitting and backed towards the door.

"I thought..." she began. Then she took a deep breath. "We've already got a bone," she said. "If you count that sheep's head in the cupboard."

"Yes, but there wasn't any blood on it. And we still haven't got a threatening message. Not on the film." My own voice was saying this. I couldn't believe it.

And I couldn't stop it.

A door slammed downstairs. The curtain billowed again.

The voices and TV sounds had stopped.

There was a chill silence.

I shuddered, and came back to myself.

Gemma was still staring at me, with a frightened, fascinated expression.

We heard footsteps coming up the stairs.

"Lizzy, don't!" breathed Gemma.

"Don't what?" I said in my normal voice.

The door handle rattled, just behind Gemma.

"Can I come in?" It was a man's voice.

"No! Don't let it..."

"Yes. Come in, Uncle Dave."

The door creaked open, slowly.

Gemma shrieked and ran to the other side of the room.

"Quite a draught in here," said my uncle's voice. Quite normally. "Have you got the window open?"

"No. I shut it after tea."

"I should shut it," said my uncle. "There's going to be a storm tonight."

He walked over to the window.

Gemma looked as if she was stuck to the wall.

He pulled the curtains apart.

A gust of icy air knifed into the room.

The bottom of the window was slightly open.

Uncle Dave grabbed the top of the sash window and heaved it down with a bang. He turned the lock in the centre.

"But I shut it when I came up!"

"That's better. Quite a draught downstairs as well. I thought I'd located it to up here."

"Where are Mum and Dad?" I managed to squeak.

He turned. "In the kitchen, I think. Why? Do you want them? I think there's some tea on the go if you want some."

"No, it's all ri - " my voice stuck in my throat again. I swallowed. "It's all right. Thanks."

"Anything the matter? You look as if you've seen a ghost."

"Yes," said Gemma faintly.

"No," I said loudly.

"No to the ghost or to the tea?" He sounded amused. "I came up to see if you'd like to play that video to me now. The programme we wanted to see is finished, so the TV's all ours."

"I've got to finish my homework," said Gemma in a rush.

Uncle Dave went on as if he hadn't heard.

"You were a bit bothered about some things you thought you hadn't filmed, so I thought now would be a good time to take a closer look and see if there's a bit of hoaxing going on, or if it can all be explained."

"Gemma," I said, "we need to know."

"I suppose so. Yes," said Gemma. She clenched and unclenched her hands at her sides.

"Where are the rest of your mates?" asked my uncle. "I thought the whole gang was here?"

"They went off home again," I said. "But it doesn't matter. We can look at the video. If you think there's a reasonable explanation, I can tell them tomorrow. Anyway," I laughed - the laugh sounded wild and strange in my ears - "Anyway, even if it is quite accidental that we've got these effects, they could be good for our film."

"There you are," said my uncle. "Let's go and put the thing on, then."

Gemma clutched at my arm as we sat together on the sofa.

My uncle fiddled with wires.

"I'll get this put onto a proper cassette for you," he said. "These tiny camcorders are all very well, but..."

The screen flickered, and the now familiar beginning of our film came into view.

ROPE TRICK

Even though we hadn't done any editing the succession of images on the first tape was very powerful. There was almost a story already. The rope, swinging significantly over the upturned stool, created just the right feel of menace. Then we saw the cracked and peeling walls, the cobwebs, the split and splintered floorboards...

"We didn't..." I began. Surely we hadn't filmed the floor Lee had fallen though?

"Shh," said my uncle.

In the next frame Ben's ponytail dangled from the rope.

"I still can't find it," choked Gemma.

Hollow rapping as the camera panned around and settled on to my horrified face.

"That's really good," said my uncle. "What did they do to you to make you look like that?"

"Wait till you see Paul," said Gemma in a tight voice.

My wound-up feelings relaxed a bit when we did see Paul. It was obvious he was only horrified about his hair. We told Uncle Dave and he laughed. "I'd have just thought it was a bit of bad acting if you hadn't told me."

The screen exploded into lines.

"Now what?" he said, puzzled.

"Oh, that's just where we changed the cassette," I said hurriedly. He looked at me hard but said nothing, just rewound the first tape and put in the second.

The teddy bear lay sprawled and mangled.

"Yuk!" said my uncle. "You do think of some

nasty ideas!"

Then the tap appeared, a slow drip, drip of water splashing red into the sink. My uncle looked closely. "Light," he muttered. "I'm still sure it's reflections off that coat."

Gemma's hand clutched my arm.

"Where's the skull?" Her voice trembled. "It was on the first..."

"I thought you said..." began my uncle at the same time.

The cupboard door creaked.

"That's a good effect..."

And the skull grinned.

I gasped. "There's blood..."

"On top of the skull. A great, red mass of it."

And as we watched, the gory mess slithered down into the blank eye socket and dripped...

Dripped down onto the shelf.

On top of a piece of paper.

The camera moved slowly in and we could just make out the words:

DEAD MEN TELL NO LIES.

Chapter 11

"So it was you!" accused Gemma in a voice of ice. "I don't know why you think I'm so stupid I can't see through you. You've had the films all the time. You've had the camera here. It's got to be one of you. Or both of you together. You've thought of this blood dripping idea before and put it on just to scare me! Well, it didn't work this time because I know!"

Visibly holding herself together she didn't wait for an answer but rushed blindly out of the house.

My mouth was still open as I heard the front door slam.

The taped film came to an end. Only the grey dotted lines of empty electronic signals rushed busily across the screen.

"I..." I began.

My uncle switched off the TV and unplugged the camcorder.

"Someone's having fun," he commented.

I was shaking all over. I knew now. It had to be my uncle playing these tricks on us. And I'd felt sorry for him, moving into a haunted house!

"How did you know?" I demanded. "Were you listening at the door?"

"Listening to what?"

He looked completely innocent, but that was the way he'd looked all the time. All those times when we'd thought there was something evil going on, and he'd simply stolen our ideas and put them onto our films. He'd admitted to setting up the rope, hadn't he?

"Listening to our ideas!"

"I hope you're not accusing me of listening at doors, Lizzy."

"How else could it have happened?" I burst out. "All these things have come onto the film since you..."

"Lizzy," he said patiently. "Even if I had eavesdropped - and I assure you I didn't - I couldn't possibly have put anything onto this film in such a short time. Are you sure you're not more adept at this video business than you're letting on? It's not a very nice trick to play on your friend, but I'm impressed by your technique."

"I didn't - I didn't!" I cried. "How could I? I'm just as much in the dark as you - or Gemma! I don't know anything about filming special effects. I just point it in the right direction, press the button and hope for the best!"

His half-smile told me that he didn't believe me.

But if it wasn't my uncle, who could it be?

My mind was in a turmoil as I watched him carefully pack Helen's camcorder away.

Helen's camcorder...

No. It couldn't be anything to do with the camcorder. The strange images on the film had come whether we used the school camcorder or Helen's. And we'd tried two different tapes.

And each time we'd played our film back something sinister had appeared on the TV screen.

I thought again about the TV - but we'd already agreed that it couldn't be the set. It didn't play about with ordinary videotapes, nor with scheduled programmes.

And even if it was the TV set, it didn't explain how a message had come over the radio.

"All right?"

My uncle stood in the doorway. I roused myself.

"Yeah, I'm all right," I told him.

"If you're scared, just shout, won't you? It's got to be one of your friends monkeying with tapes. Swapping them when you're not looking. I should think up a few leading questions if I were you!"

Yes. It had to be that. It was all perfectly possible. I felt a great wave of relief surge through my body.

"And the radio message would have been really easy, I should think," I said, warming to his idea. "I mean, if you're good at playing about with electronics - computers and telephones and virtual reality and all that..."

"Real reality's real enough for me," said my uncle with a little laugh. "But you're right. Someone who can play about with these things might...I don't know. I'm too old to learn about that sort of thing."

"It hasn't got anything to do with age!" I

protested. "For heaven's sake, I don't know how these things work either, and I'm only fifteen! But I'm not that good at anything really."

You could tell it had been Monday again. And it had been a long, long day.

"Nonsense!" said my uncle sharply. "But it certainly does take a certain kind of mind to be good at things like computers and to understand how virtual reality works. I wonder..."

"Yes?" I was eager for any kind of reasonable explanation.

Any explanation, except for the unreasonable one I dreaded.

"Perhaps a mixture of technology and psychology could be the answer. Someone knows what you could be thinking..."

"Uncle Dave, that's really unnerving!"

"No, but think about it," he insisted. "Somebody puts the germ of an idea in your head - so sneakily that you don't even notice - and before you know it, you've said what they want you to say."

"And if it's something they can put onto a film beforehand and quickly swap it..."

"You've got the idea. Exactly!" said my uncle triumphantly.

I could see it now. All those things I couldn't understand, like the idea of the blood-soaked bone.

It wasn't even the kind of bone I'd thought about in the first place, but the old sheep skull.

If you reasoned things out, it wasn't so hard

to understand. It would explain that compulsion I'd had to talk about blood dripping from the bone.

In my head I could still see those images which appeared on the screen: the thick, oozing gash of red, slowly slipping down from the stark white skull...

But who could be messing about with these tapes? Could it possibly be my uncle? Could he be giving me hints that it was him all the time? In spite of what he said, I knew he did know quite a bit about computers and electronic technology.

But why was he still keen to scare the wits out of us?

There'd be no point in asking him straight out. His hints about how it could have been done might be a challenge to me. Maybe he'd pointed me in the right direction - shown me how to look for the answer to the mystery.

Maybe he had a bet on with people at work. Something like that.

He'd hoped we'd suss him out when he set up that first rope trick. Then again when he'd sent the local radio message. But we hadn't caught on. And then with my parents getting worried and Gemma going hysterical he'd begun to think perhaps it was time we got round to working it all out.

The hints, perhaps, were so that I could catch him at it the next time.

I wondered how much time was left before

the bet ran out.

"I think you're right," I said slowly. My hands, which I didn't know had been clenched, unfolded themselves just as slowly. "I'll keep my eyes open."

"I will, too," said my uncle. "It's getting a bit too much of a good thing, isn't it? But hadn't you better get off to bed? School tomorrow."

"I suppose I'd better. Goodnight, then."

"I hope my suggestions mean you get a better night's sleep," he said. "Don't worry, I'll switch off the lights."

"I'll take the tapes and Helen's camcorder up with me," I said. There was no way I was going to leave them in the sitting room for my Uncle Dave to mess about with. "I'll pack them in my bag ready for tomorrow."

And I'd sleep with my school bag so that there was no way anyone could get at it!

I woke in the night.

No wonder! The school backpack was still digging into my side. I felt for the cassettes. Still there, under my History homework, and the camcorder. Its shape was unmistakable.

With all that lot digging into me, I couldn't go back to sleep again. The window banged and rattled in the wind. And in-between the gusts I could hear the thumps of conkers falling from the big horse-chestnut tree at the side of our garden. The window rattled again and my curtain billowed.

It couldn't be open again! I'd checked it was

shut before I went to sleep.

I tried to pull myself together. Use your reason, Lizzy.

It had opened by itself before. Nothing supernatural but a broken sash cord. Our house is old - it creaks and moves at the best of times. In windy weather you can imagine all sorts of things. But there was a reasonable explanation for everything.

Wasn't there?

With the school bag digging into my back I lay and tried to work out a reasonable explanation for everything that had happened. Then I could challenge my uncle tomorrow and win the bet for him. Or whatever it was.

First - the swinging rope.

Uncle Dave had set up the scene in the cottage. He'd told us that. It would have been easy for him to either set up a draught to make the rope swing, or to switch cassettes before we watched our movie.

And Ben's hair. If Gemma really had put it into her backpack with the camera, he could have taken it out and filmed the scene with it tied to the rope.

The teddy bear. That was even more obvious. Uncle Dave had hidden the toy in the skip and planted the idea of looking there in Lee's mind.

The red in the sink could be explained - as Uncle Dave had said - by the reflections from Helen's red anorak.

And the blood red bath water?

Maybe it was simply what my father had thought it was: the water board's roadworks contaminating the water.

But in that case, why hadn't our water run red? We were in the same street. On the same water main.

I had forgotten to ask my father what the water board had said when he rang today.

If in fact he had called them today.

I tossed and turned in my bed, knocking my hips against the school bag, hearing the window bang and shudder in the wind.

It could all be perfectly reasonable, but there was one thing that I couldn't explain away.

I'd had a feeling there was going to be something wrong with this movie before we'd even started it. Before Uncle Dave came to stay. Before we'd even heard of the cottage.

There was something evil about the whole idea. Just the idea.

It was nothing to do with Uncle Dave. He'd been trying to reassure us, to make sense of it for himself as well. Trying to take away all our fears by explaining everything in a rational way.

I thought back to where I'd left him downstairs.

That look he'd given me.

He wasn't anxious that we should find out for ourselves. Afraid we wouldn't discover his tricks in time for him to win some kind of bet.

He was just plain afraid.

And then, with relief, I thought of another way this could be happening.

Maybe it was something to do with our minds - though not in the way Uncle Dave had suggested.

Maybe our minds, focusing together, could influence what we filmed. Maybe the evil was coming from all of us, without us realising it.

In that case, if we all thought of something good, this is what would come out on the film. If we kept evil out of our minds we could change it easily, quickly, exactly as our minds had changed our real film into something we had all wanted but didn't have the know-how to do.

The wind died down. My backpack moved itself so that the corners weren't digging into my back and shoulders, fatigue overcame me and I slept.

For the second time, when I called for Gemma she wasn't ready.

Or didn't want to walk to school with me.

I tried to talk to her during the morning, but she kept avoiding all of us.

The boys didn't want to talk either. They both went off very enthusiastically to join the football club at the end of the morning session.

A thing they'd never wanted to do before.

The bench was empty. I didn't want to sit there by myself. As I stood, uncertain what to do, where to eat my packed lunch, a group of giggling first years moved onto it, looking round shiftily in case one of us came along and yelled at them to get off.

I turned away, feeling sick with sadness.

Whatever evil there was in this film of ours, it had broken up our friendly group.

"Where shall we go?"

It was Helen. She moved to my side and walked with me towards the cafeteria and the coke machine.

"I had an idea," I blurted out.

"Yes?" Helen's eyes snapped alive. For the second time, I wondered why I'd never noticed the way they went so strangely blank from time to time.

"I think we're making these things happen on our horror movie."

Her eyes went dead again. "So?"

"So if we think of a different kind of story - you know, an ordinary kind of story. Like, perhaps, the story of the people who used to live at the cottage." I'd been thinking it out all morning. "We haven't got time to find out for real, but we do know about them going to Canada, and coming back to find the place deserted and sad. I mean, we could do a bit about their lives here, and then the father getting a job in Canada, and..." I was warming to my idea now. "They could look round at all the things they were leaving behind, and then we could do a bit when they come back and find the house empty and falling down..."

My voice trailed away lamely. I could see

Helen wasn't impressed.

"Well...it was just an idea," I finished unhappily.

Helen shrugged. "We could go and see," she said. "A different game, you mean?"

My stomach lurched uncomfortably. "Game?"

"Rope Trick," she said. "What it said on the radio," she reminded me.

"If it's our minds playing games, well - yes, I suppose so."

"Sounds a bit boring," said Helen.

Suddenly her eyes were quite normal.

"Boring, perhaps, but a lot safer," I said. "I'm really scared of this film, Helen. I want to do something before - before one of us ends up on the end of that rope!"

Chapter 12

"Well? Had a good day?"

My uncle was there in the kitchen when I got home after school. His eyes were still anxious, enquiring. I was pretty certain now that it wasn't Uncle Dave who had tampered with our tapes, but I had to make sure, one last time.

"It isn't you, is it?"

"Me? I've told you. I don't know anything about technology. It's enough of a headache knowing which bits of my house need renovating."

"Could I - we - go again? Just one more time?"

He looked even more anxious. "Are you sure you ought? You mean, all of you?"

"Well, in fact only me and Helen. The others are - well, the others are busy," I finished defiantly.

"Are you sure you want to?"

Was there a warning in his glance?

"We've got something to finish. Are you going to be there tonight?"

"Sorry - I've got a meeting tonight. The builders will probably still be there, but maybe only until six. What time were you thinking of?"

"There's a bus at half past five," I said. "We won't get in their way. It was only to..." I didn't know whether to tell him about my new idea. But surely nothing bad could happen if we talked about such an ordinary story.

But there were things I could ask, without risking anything.

"Can you tell me about these people, Uncle Dave?" I began, watching him closely. I was still not absolutely, one hundred per cent sure. "The people who went to Canada. Do you know anything more about them? I mean, if we don't finish our horror story, we might be able to do something about their lives, mightn't we?"

I swear the relief on his face was genuine.

"The problem is I don't know much more than I've already told you," he said, reaching for the kettle and filling it from the tap. "But you could ask the neighbours."

"Neighbours? I didn't know you had any!"

He grinned. "Not neighbours like here, but they're only across a couple of fields. They knew the Dunstons fairly well, I think. You need to be neighbourly when you're out in the country - even if it's not that far out."

Neighbours. Even better. I could film them talking about the Dunstons, find out why Mr Dunston had chosen to go to Canada and why they hadn't managed to sell their house until now.

"Uncle Dave..."

The kettle boiled and he threw a couple of tea-bags into the pot before showing he'd heard me.

"You said it was because...because of it being too far away. But it's not, is it? I mean, we can get there on the bus, easy as anything. You've got to tell me the truth - it was because the house was haunted, wasn't it?"

"Lizzy," said my uncle, warningly. "You're making things up again. I've told you everything just the way the estate agent told it to me. And that's everything I know. All right? If there are any ghosts, I don't know anything about them, okay? Besides," he laughed as he reboiled the water and poured it into the teapot, "the men who are doing the damp-proof course will find anything you might think is walled up in there!"

"Don't!" I said sharply. Don't let anything come into my mind, just in case somebody - the somebody I think can read my mind - somebody catches hold of the idea and makes it happen.

I made myself think of tea, and biscuits, and the supper I was to cook for my parents and uncle.

"Is spaghetti bolognese all right?" I asked him. It was a meal I could prepare in my sleep. It was about all I could do successfully! With other, more complicated things, I often missed out some essential ingredient. Or cooked it for too long or not long enough.

"Can I do anything?"

"No problem," I said. Think about spag bog. Keep my mind on onions, tomatoes... "It won't take long. Go and have your tea by the TV. I think there's some cake left."

"Good," said my uncle greedily. He found the tin and sliced a hunk off.

I waited for him to go through to the sitting

room, then began frying onions and minced beef. Like I said, I can do it in my sleep. I didn't have to think enough to blot out the other, disturbing things which kept floating into my mind.

I had to keep trying to push away the idea of the man walled up under the plaster.

Diced carrots. Oregano. Bay leaf.

The scent of frying onions filled the kitchen and I reached for the garlic.

Garlic.

It kept away vampires.

Perhaps it would keep away the ghosts in the house.

If there were any ghosts.

Ghosts or - or whatever it was that was shaping my mind and making these images appear on our videotape.

I grabbed a whole, unused bulb of garlic and pushed it deep down into my jeans pocket. Then I shoved a heap of paper tissues on top of it, and left the corner of one sticking out, so that it looked as if that was all I had in there.

Mrs Sandis was a pleasant, plump woman with the sort of giggle that makes you want to laugh even if you haven't seen anything funny.

"Oh, yes, they were lovely neighbours," she told Helen and I. "I was really sorry to see them go off to Canada."

"But why did they go?" I insisted.

"I think Derek always had a yen to go to Canada," she said. "He'd got some distant relations out in Vancouver, I think that's where he said. But the job was this side of Canada so I can't see that they'll meet up that often!" And she giggled again, making both Helen and I laugh.

"There wasn't - isn't - anything - sort of - funny about the cottage, is there?" I asked.

"Funny? What sort of funny?"

"Well..." I felt a bit silly now, asking about ghosts. "Well, anything, sort of, supernatural."

"No chance," said Mrs Sandis, and she giggled again. "I'd like to see a ghost hanging about in this part of the country! No, we're all too sensible here to have ghosts."

I didn't laugh this time. The word 'hanging' stayed in my ears.

"Besides," Mrs Sandis went on, "if there were any ghosts, my two would have found them. Always playing over there, they are."

"Children?" Helen's voice was sharp with interest.

"One of each, a boy and a girl. I've told them now it's sold they mustn't go over there any more, but they still do. I must tell your uncle to shoo them away."

"What do they do?" I could hear the strain in my own voice.

"Do? Well, what do children do? I never know what they get up to. They're safe enough around here. There's no ponds or anything for them to fall into, no quarries to fall down, no forests to get lost in. Just boring fields!" And she chuckled again. "They've enjoyed making up their little stories in your uncle's house. Well - not in - I don't think they ever found their way in - but in the outhouses and around. Though my husband did say they were to stop playing in the outhouses, now the roof's beginning to cave in. It's a bit dangerous. Is your uncle going to repair them or pull them down?"

"I - oh, I - er - I don't know," I confessed. Children. Two children. Playing round - or perhaps in - the house. Had they left something there which was affecting our film? Were they wrapping some kind of evil influence round the house?

No. Surely not. Not children.

But it was only too possible. Two kids 'making up little stories' their mother had said. She said she didn't know what they got up to.

I could see it all. They'd been brought up here. They knew exactly where to hide. They'd probably listened to everything we'd talked about and decided to improve on it. It would be easy for a clever kid.

Easier still for a kid who had some kind of supernatural powers. I kept trying to believe that the images on our film could have been done by anyone with the right know-how, but underneath I think I always knew that it just wasn't possible. The only way anyone could have made our film or could have instigated the copycat events, was by using powers that we didn't understand. A paranormal power perhaps? Whatever it was, it was a power that people were frightened of.

I pulled myself together. We needed a nice, uncomplicated story. Perhaps these two kids would let us film them, playing their nice, uncomplicated games.

"How old are they?" I asked casually.

"The kids? Simon's ten and Samantha's eight. Want to say hello to them, if I can find them? Since you'll be nearly neighbours, so to speak."

Without waiting for a reply, she went to the door and bawled the children's names in the sort of voice which would carry over several fields. Helen looked at me and grinned.

Then her face straightened again and she looked thoughtful.

I felt the garlic in my pocket. I wondered if anyone could smell it.

I looked at Helen. Was she thinking the same as me?

"It couldn't be them, could it?" I whispered.

"They might have strung up the rope, if your uncle hadn't already confessed to it," said Helen. "Think they might have found Lee's teddy bear and hung it from the rope?"

"Kids? They wouldn't do that. Would they?"

"Pinch it, or string it up?"

I shuddered. "Either."

"I don't know," said Helen. "I did some pretty nasty things to my toys when I was that age. Didn't you?"

Did I? "Yes, I suppose I did - I beat the life out of my toy panda once when I thought my brother was getting more attention than me."

"Any of us could do it." Her voice was insistent. "Anyone."

"What are you getting at?" I asked curiously. She shrugged. "Oh - nothing. But..."

"Helen - do you know something I don't? Do you know who's been at our tapes? Helen - tell me!"

But from behind the house peeped the faces of two grubby kids.

"Where's Mum?" asked the tallest one, the boy. Simon.

"Yelling for you," said Helen, grinning.

"Oh, I know that. You can hear her miles off. We just wait till she's had to go a really long way!"

He laughed. So did his sister. They came closer to us. "You the new neighbours?" asked the girl, who must have been Samantha.

"Not really," I said. "My uncle is."

"Are there any children?"

"No," I told them. "Why?"

"We thought...well, we just thought there were."

So that they could torment them?

"Did you know the children who were here before?" I asked.

Samantha giggled just like her mother. "They're grown-ups! They're not children. They came to see us."

Of course. It had been a long time.

"Would you like to have children at the cottage?"

"It'd be someone to play with," shrugged Simon. "We've got some good games."

Like tying a bunch of hair to a rope? Like hanging a mutilated teddy bear? Like hiding skulls in cupboards and dripping blood from them?

"What sort of games?" I asked casually.

"Oh - murder games," he grinned.

My feet went cold.

"I think - I think it's time we went," I said to Helen. "It's nearly time for the bus."

"Hang on," said Helen. She was staring at Simon. "What kind of murder games?"

Her eyes had gone that frightening blank again.

"Murder games? Oh, you know - 'Murder in the Dark'. We go out there and creep around. It's good now it's beginning to get dark. Then we scream. To scare people. Well - to scare each other, really. There aren't any people."

"Only the builders, and they've gone by the time we get back from school," said Samantha.

"Don't," I said.

"Don't what?" Helen's voice had gone silky smooth.

"Don't give them any more ideas." My voice cracked with strain.

"It's all right," said Simon, grinning at Helen. "We don't get that frightened. Not any more."

"He used to give me nightmares when I was

little," volunteered Samantha. "But he doesn't now. I can scare him worse than he can scare me."

"What does he hate most?" Helen's tongue darted out to lick her top lip. Just like a snake. My legs seemed frozen solid. I couldn't move.

"I'm not telling you," said Samantha.

"She wants to do all the scaring herself!" laughed Simon.

"I could give you some ideas," breathed Helen.

"No, Helen!"

My heart pounded. I didn't want her to encourage them into anything else. I didn't like the way these children seemed to derive pleasure out of frightening people. Did they know what they were doing? Did they know they could frighten people to death?

Horrifyingly I saw the image of a crushed body, imprisoned in stone, dripping blood into the pipes of the house like the veins in a body.

"Helen," I begged, "please don't give them any more ideas. Let's go - now!"

"But I don't want to go now. I'm having fun."

Her eyes moved slowly to meet mine. They were still blank, as if there was no one there. No warm, living, breathing person inside. But there was an intelligence there. A mind that knew what it was doing.

ROPE TRICK

Chapter 13

"There you are!"

Helen shook her blonde hair, my legs unstuck, and the two kids turned and grinned at their mother.

"They're little brats!" continued Mrs Sandis. "They wait till I'm so hoarse I can hardly speak, then they turn up." She flung her arms round them both and hugged them close. The kids turned and grinned at her.

"We want to make sure you get plenty of exercise," explained Simon.

"Oh - you!" She pretended to slap them both, but they dodged out of the way and ran, laughing, into the house.

They were just nice, uncomplicated kids.

But Helen was trying to poison their minds.

I don't know why I hadn't seen it before. Everything came to me with blinding clarity. It was Helen, of course, who had thought of doing a horror movie in the first place. Helen who had kept nagging at us to carry on with it, when most of us had become sickened at the thought.

I had to protect these kids, even if it was too late for us.

"Well, thanks anyway. We've got to go," I said.

There was no way I could bring Helen here again.

I wanted to get back to my own kind of

normality where I could control what I did. Where I could trust people. My family - even Uncle Dave, now that I knew for sure he had nothing to do with the strange images on our videotapes.

And I knew I wanted to get as far away from Helen as possible.

We waited in silence for the bus. Light was fading. Clouds built up behind the hilly rise of stubbly fields. Some of the fields were already ploughed and dark.

I didn't like being near her. My body ached with holding itself straight, to appear quite ordinary.

I saw the bus coming. I've never been so glad to see a bus in all my life. It meant people, real people. People with eyes that smiled, eyes that flashed with anger, eyes that wept.

Not eyes which were totally, totally blank.

"You can't escape, you know," said Helen.

My heart lurched. I felt so frightened I couldn't move.

"I don't know what you're talking about." Perhaps if I refused to admit anything was happening it wouldn't happen.

I watched the bus crawling slow as a slug along the country road. Behind the high fields the clouds were stained garish purple and orange.

The bus seemed to disappear as the road wound through hedges. My stomach knotted itself tight. Would it ever appear again? Was I trapped, here, with Helen?

I could feel her presence like a cold block of ice. I shivered and hugged my arms round me to try and warm myself, but the cold went right through me.

I couldn't bear it. Time seemed to stand still.

"Why? Why?" I cried. My words fell thin and sharp on empty air.

"Why what?"

Helen's voice seemed quite normal. I risked looking at her.

Her eyes were warm, matching the smile on her mouth.

I took a deep, shuddering breath, and the bus suddenly approached us from round a corner, its engine hot and heavy and noisy.

"I was going to say why doesn't the darned bus come!" I said with huge relief.

"It has," said Helen. "So why don't we just get on?"

We climbed aboard and flopped down into the nearest double seat.

"What a stink!" I said. It was a lovely smell - diesel, sweat, somebody's old fish and chip paper. It was life!

"I meant to say," said Helen chattily, she looked me full in the eyes, and I shuddered again at the momentary blankness in them, "talking of stinks. Excuse me if I'm being personal, but you've been stinking of garlic all evening."

It was a warning.

A warning not to try and stop her from

whatever she wanted to do.

"You've got to promise not to do anything involving those kids," I said.

"They're only mucking around," said Helen. "They liked making people scared."

"Yes, but..."

Supposing I wasn't right?

"But?"

"Not your sort of being scared," I said bluntly.

She raised her pale eyebrows. "You mean because I can watch horror movies without having nightmares for weeks afterwards?"

"I mean, I think your idea of fun is sick."

There. I'd said it. Straight out.

"You might regret saying that," she said sulkily.

What had I done? Lost a friend? Or told a she-devil that I knew what she was up to?

As the bus droned back into town I had panic regrets. She sat with her hair draped over her face, the way she always did when she was upset. Then she shook it back and I could see tears staining her cheeks.

"Helen - I'm..."

"Don't say you're sorry," she said fiercely. "You know you're not. You know you meant it."

"I don't know whether I did or not," I told her wretchedly.

"Just leave me alone," she said, and sniffed.

If she'd left it at that, I would have believed her, believed she had nothing to do with the horrible changes in our film.

130

But as we got off the bus I turned, my face pleading... and met a glare of such hatred that it sent a chill down my spine.

I knew I had to persuade the others to scrap our movie.

I didn't think it would be so hard.

"Sorry," said Mr Parker on Wednesday. "I've got other classes which need to use the equipment, you know. Can't make exceptions. You'll just have to make do with what you've got."

Time had run out.

We had to do the cutting of our videotape during our lunch times because there was no more time in class. All this part of our coursework had to be finished by the beginning of next week, when we'd show our films to each other in the Media Studies lesson.

"No," said Gemma.

"But you've got to," said Lee. "Come on, Gemma - we've spent such a lot of time on this, and it's really good, I know it is."

Gemma glared at me. She still wouldn't talk to me, or walk with me to school.

"You're sure Lizzy won't have changed it all again?" she said bitingly.

"It wasn't Lizzy," said Helen.

I waited with bated breath for her to tell Gemma who it was.

"We've just imagined it all. We've got caught up in our own horror story," went on Helen. "We really did set up all those images, you know."

"But how come...?" began Paul.

"Come off it, Helen," said Lee, but you could tell he was uncertain.

"Sure. Don't you remember?" said Helen.

And the way she said it you would have thought she was right.

If you didn't know otherwise.

I wanted to tell them all about Helen, but every time I opened my mouth it was as if she knew what I was going to say, and interrupted me. And made it all seem perfectly natural.

I'd go round and see the boys this evening, I vowed.

"Paul and I are going to that new film at the Lighthouse tonight," said Lee. "Fabulous Western – you coming?"

"Westerns! Me?" said Gemma. "You have to be joking!"

I clutched at the garlic in my pocket.

I'd go and see Gemma, then. I'd make her talk to me.

"Anyway, my Mum's taking us out for a meal, as it's Ben's birthday," she went on.

I glanced at Helen.

She gave me a long, considering stare, and a little smile played about the corner of her mouth.

I wanted to yell out at everyone - "Don't listen to her!" - but the words stuck in my throat.

"So what about it, Gemma?" said Lee. "I reckon Helen's right. We lost your brother's ponytail, and made up a story to make us believe someone else had lost it."

"Yes, that's what it was," said Gemma.

It was like a zombie talking.

I dug my thumbnail into one of the hard cloves of the garlic, deep in my pocket. "Suppose it's spiders next time!" I said loudly.

There. The garlic had worked. I could speak. I opened my mouth to say more but Helen interrupted in that soft, reasonable, new voice.

"Lizzy - you know Gemma hates them. Come on, don't be difficult."

Me? Difficult! I stared, panic-stricken, at my friends. "But don't you realise...?" I tried to begin.

It wouldn't come out. I began to cough. That sort of embarrassing cough where you just can't stop and you splutter and spit all over the place.

"I'll come with you to get a drink, Lizzy."

"No!"

No, please no. I don't want Helen to come with me. Why don't the rest of you come as well, then...

But I didn't have any choice. I couldn't speak. Every time I began my words turned into another terrible, retching cough.

She came to the toilets with me. There was a fountain in the corner. She pressed the lever and pushed my head into the jet of drinking water.

I was breathing water. I gasped and retched and spluttered.

Suddenly the pressure went from my shoulder and I heard Gemma.

"Is she all right?"

I heard Helen laughing, telling Gemma

about the bulb of garlic in my pocket. "I don't know why she's got it there, but you can smell it on her fingernails. I bet that's what made her choke! Shall we get rid of it for her?"

Of course, Helen couldn't touch it herself. It must be making her feel quite ill! Good!

But Gemma was my friend. My best friend. She wouldn't do anything I didn't want her to.

"What have you brought that to school for, Lizzy?" Helen's voice was still hatefully friendly. "Shall Gemma get rid of it for you?"

"No, you mustn't. It's...!"

But I felt Gemma's hand tear at my pocket and grab the bulb of garlic.

Helen was totally in control now.

Her eyes were blank and unemotional. And I could see Gemma's eyes clouding over too.

"Gemma," I whispered. "Be careful! She's got us all in her power!"

"Come on, Lizzy. You're having bad dreams. It's all because of that silly nonsense you put on the tapes."

Was this my friend Gemma talking?

"But I've thought about it, and you know, I think it's really good. I was annoyed with you for scaring me, but the pictures will make a really great horror movie."

My throat was paralysed. I couldn't speak. Water ran down from my hair and dripped down my face.

I heard the bell for the end of the lunch break.

"Come on. Let's clean you up. You can't go

back into the class like that."

"I'll stay with her, Gemma," offered Helen. "Just tell them we'll be there in a minute."

No!

It was registration time. Suddenly the place was full of girls, making a last minute visit to the loo.

We had to be in class. Now.

I couldn't move. Still.

In the clamour, Helen pushed her face right up against mine.

"I haven't finished yet. And you won't stop me. You can't stop me. You know you can't. You can load yourself up with garlic, and you won't be able to stop me."

She smiled.

I hated that smile.

We had to work at it through Thursday and Friday lunch times.

Every time we ran the tape through the machine on Thursday I waited for something different to happen. But it was all the same as before.

And after a time it didn't seem so scary. We got used to the mutilated teddy bear hanging from his rope. We argued about how we would arrange everything. We learned how to use the cutting machine and how to stick the pieces together.

My terror was worse. I couldn't speak, or tell anyone about Helen. I couldn't tell my parents and I couldn't tell my friends.

None of them would believe me if I had.

All I could do was keep a bulb of garlic in my pocket, all the time. Maybe Helen was right - that I couldn't stop her from doing anything she wanted to do. But if I could delay things, at least we might stop her doing anything to our film.

I was afraid of what or who she planned to hang from that rope.

She didn't seem to have done anything as yet.

And we were all friends together again.

I think we were friends.

It was hard to tell.

There was a kind of barrier between us all, and yet on the surface everything seemed perfectly all right.

"We still haven't got a proper story," I said. "We know what it's all about, but I don't think it's explained properly."

"We need a voice-over," decided Lee.

"We need a script," I said sarcastically. "I said that, right at the beginning. I said none of us was any good at stories."

I'd said a lot of things I wished I hadn't said.

If only we'd thought of another story in the first place.

Like the story of the Dunstons.

But there was no point in wishing that.

"Who's going to be the voice-over?" asked Paul.

"Do you fancy yourself as an actor, Paul?"

"Well, I'm in it, aren't I? Yeah - how about me telling the story from the boy in the story's point of view?"

"I was just having my hair permed when..." mocked Gemma.

Almost normal. I began to hope we could be real people again, with minds of our own.

"Lee can do it," said Helen.

Her words fell into the conversation like a cold block of ice.

There was no discussion. We knew Lee would do it.

"Well..." said Lee uncertainly after what seemed long minutes of silence between us.

"Yeah, Lee will do it."

We nodded. And looked at each other. Knowing there was something terribly wrong.

Knowing that we weren't in control of ourselves any more.

I felt the bulb of garlic in my pocket.

Perhaps if we all carried some, she wouldn't be able to get at us so easily.

But she could get at my voice. There was no way I could talk. No way I could tell the others what I desperately wanted to tell them.

And I couldn't discuss anything with my Uncle Dave. Mum told me he'd had to go away to Leeds or somewhere, on business for a couple of days.

"He'll be back at the weekend," she said when she arrived home on Thursday night.

"But he left a message somewhere - now, where is it?"

"A message? For me?"

"I can't think what...I put it down only seconds ago..."

It was my Mum all over. So efficient at so many things, and yet she could never remember where she put things. We were always having to search for her watch, or her handbag.

I didn't find it funny now.

"Try," I urged. "Where did he give it to you? Where were you? Did he say anything?"

She rubbed her hands distractedly through her hair. "I'm sorry, Lizzy, but I simply can't remember. It'll turn up before too long, I'm sure. Things always do."

"Did he say anything?"

"I don't think so. Only to give it to you. And that he'd be back on Friday night."

Was he trying to warn me about something?

He'd already tried, that evening. All his talk about psychology and things added up. Only there wasn't any technical know-how needed to change everything on our videotapes.

Only the mind of someone evil.

If only he was here. Together we might have been able to work out some way of stopping Helen from using her dark powers to make something really terrible happen.

I tried to reason myself out of my panic.

If anything was going to happen, it would happen next Monday, when we played our films to the rest of the class.

Uncle Dave would be back on Friday. I could talk to him then. Tell him what I knew, and ask for his help.

I had to be content with that.

I took a whole bagful of garlic with me to school next day.

And slipped a bulb into the bags of each of my friends.

Helen sidled up to me at first break.

"I'm not a vampire, you know," she said.

"What? I don't know what you're talking about!"

My heart was banging against my ribs.

"I said I'm not a vampire. It's been a lot of fun playing with you and that garlic, but it doesn't work. Sorry."

Her smile made me shudder.

"It's for cookery," I said stupidly.

"Sure it is," said Helen, and drifted away again.

I had a feeling that if we got the film finished without changing anything else I would have won. If we didn't talk about anything else in the story, but just left it as it was.

We worked in silence at lunch time. None of us wanted to say anything. We all knew it would be such a huge relief when it was finished.

Except Helen.

But Helen said nothing either.

I began to think that perhaps the powerful smell and influence of the garlic I'd hidden all around us was having some effect, in spite of what she said.

There was ten minutes left before the end of the break. We were nearly finished. Lee's voice-over had gone without a hitch. There was just time to play the whole thing through.

We sat back, while Paul put our beautifully structured tape into the large holder and pushed it into the video playback machine.

The horror story began. Lee's voice spoke quietly over the images of the rope and stopped to let Paul's and my horrified faces speak for themselves. We'd fitted in the best of the knocking sounds onto our soundtrack and our faces looked really great as the camera panned round the walls, so you knew where the sounds were coming from.

Suddenly Gemma burst out, "I know how we can end our story!"

"No! No, Gemma!" I grabbed her arm.

"Shut up!" Lee's voice was hoarse.

"Gemma, stop it!" Paul tried to push his hand across her mouth.

"What do you think you're doing?"

Mr Parker's loudest voice rang in our ears. He stood in the doorway, watching us fight to keep Gemma from saying anything.

"Sir, we've got to stop..."

Mr Parker strode across the floor.

In front of us the screen flickered to the end of our story. But Gemma pulled herself away from Paul and I and yelled, "We end up with the body of one of the children. Swinging on the rope!"

As the film drew inexorably to a close, I recognised the face of the youngest of those two neighbouring children. Samantha. Hanging from the rope.

And saw the gleam of triumph on Helen's face.

There was a slim - a very slim - chance. I knew my uncle would be at home as he had an appointment with the builders that afternoon. That part of my mind was crystal clear. But I don't remember running out of the classroom or out of the school grounds. I just remember crashing into the house and seeing Uncle Dave's astonished face as I grabbed his arm and screamed out at him.

"She's made it happen! I knew she would. We've got to go back. We've got to go now!"

Seeing the terrible panic in my face, Uncle Dave grabbed his car keys. He drove out of town and along the country road as fast as he dared, while I choked out my suspicions of Helen and how the last, terrifying image had appeared on the TV screen.

The cottage seemed deserted but my heart sank when I saw the children's bicycles, flung carelessly into the high weeds of the garden.

My uncle turned the heavy key in the lock and we rushed through the dark passageway into the kitchen.

The rope dangled, and underneath it, her head tipped back so that her face looked up at the ceiling, was the unmistakable figure of

Samantha, her feet on a wobbly wooden stool...

She turned her head and looked at us with shock and guilt.

"I *said* we shouldn't!" said Simon's voice from the barely open window. Samantha jumped and scrambled to the floor.

"What on earth do you think you're doing?" My uncle could barely contain his anger.

"You left these things lying about, so we thought it might be fun to muck about with them." Samantha was about to continue, but stopped uncertainly, looking at my ashen face.

"Was it you?" I blurted out. "Did you set it up for our camera?"

"Camera?" It was obvious from their faces that they didn't know anything about our camcorder filming.

"We found them after you'd gone and thought we'd play a trick on you."

"Well you've certainly done that," said Uncle Dave. "But I think these tricks have gone as far as I'm going to let them. Firstly, I don't want you using my cottage as your playground, and secondly, we'll see what your mother has to say when she finds out about your antics."

So saying, he hustled us all back into his car and dropped the children off. I waited nervously in the car, cringing as he ranted and raved at Mrs Sandis on the doorstep. A few minutes later, we were driving quickly back towards the school.

"Come on... I want to have a word with your

Mr Parker about Helen. It seems to me that she could do with a few disciplinary words." I followed Uncle Dave into the school building, past groups of pupils thronging their way to the buses. The bell had gone and the last lesson of the day was over. I half hoped that Parkie had left for the day so that I could try and calm my uncle down myself, but as luck would have it, we walked bang into him marching towards the staff room.

In the office, I sat and listened as Uncle Dave recounted all the upsets caused by his innocent Media Studies project, nodding and chipping in to their conversation when asked. I was worrying about Helen and how I'd face her when all this had gone public. She was bound to try and seek revenge. My hands sweated nervously and my stomach churned.

"Well, thank you for drawing this affair to my attention. I shall be speaking to the Head - and Lizzy, don't worry about a thing." Parkie smiled at me reassuringly but it didn't stop the sick feeling in my stomach. Reading my mind, my uncle put his arm round me and suggested we go home and put the kettle on.

After a cup of tea and a chocolate biscuit I was beginning to feel better.

"What will happen to Helen? I mean, she's going to be furious when she gets a reprimand from the Head and I'm worried...well..."

"You mean, what if she lets her over-active imagination take over again?" asked Uncle Dave.

"She isn't going to get the chance. After what we discussed this afternoon I think you'll find that Helen won't be troubling you anymore."

The next day at school, a special assembly was held. Helen was conspicuously absent and I'd spent most of the first half hour explaining to the others what had happened after I'd charged out of the classroom so dramatically the day before. After the usual announcements and notices, the Head stood up and addressed us all. He explained how a certain Media Studies Project had led to one pupil being suspended owing to "reprehensible and irresponsible behaviour," endangering and frightening other pupils in the class. There was a lot of nudging and whispering, and Gemma and I exchanged glances of surprise and relief.

As we filed out afterwards I thought I saw Helen's parents walking out of the main building. Grabbing Gemma by the arm we ran over to the glass doors, just in time to see them climbing into the car. In the passenger seat there was the unmistakable figure of Helen, her curtain of blonde hair covering her face, the way she always wore it when she was upset...or could she be ashamed?

"Come on Lizzy. It's over now," said Gemma, trying to steer me back to the classroom. I took one last look at the car as it swept past the doors and shivered as the blonde curtain of hair parted and the face beneath it saw me, and mouthed the words "Dead men tell no lies."